DEAD IN THE WATER

A gripping detective thriller full of suspense

PETER TICKLER

Published 2015 by Joffe Books, London.

www.joffebooks.com

© Peter Tickler

ISBN-13: 978-1517359355

Chapter 1

It was barely 6 a.m. The cloudless sky promised another scorching day. A slight breeze ruffled the tops of the trees dotted along the Thames. It was long after dawn, but the birds were still chorusing as if their lives depended on it. Not that Doug Mullen noticed. His heart and head were both pounding so hard that he felt as though they might explode at any moment and he would slip ingloriously into oblivion. The sprightly jog with which he had departed his Iffley Road flat had long since become a laboured movement of reluctant legs. He cursed himself for allowing his fitness levels to decline so far. The only benefit of inflicting this torture on himself at such a ridiculous hour — he was, after all, too far gone to enjoy this blissful post-dawn period of the day — was that there were no people around to observe his embarrassing performance. He was heading back towards the city of Oxford, having reached Sandford lock in record time. Not that his record time was anything which your average forty-year-old would have been proud of, but it had taken its toll on Mullen and as he stumbled under the ring-road his legs finally refused to obey any more orders from his brain. He stopped and bent down gasping, hands on his knees, and wondered whether he was going to be sick.

To his right the River Thames ran smooth and untroubled. To his left, dense foliage had given way to a tree-fringed grass field. And in front of him lay an uprooted oak tree, sprawled across the path and into the river. A minute passed before he raised himself upright. He grabbed a branch of the oak, conscious of the unsteadiness in his legs. And then, quite suddenly, he saw the body.

He had seen dead bodies before, but only in places where you expect to see them, which was why (presumably) he now vomited forth what little food there was in his stomach. However, if his short spell in the army had taught him anything, it was not to freeze in a crisis. He pulled his mobile out of his pocket, rang 999 and reported the body. As soon as that was done, he made his way along the horizontal trunk of the oak in order to get a closer look.

Part of him knew that he should leave the woman there, floating face down in the water, long hair extended across the surface. The tree was effectively holding her prisoner and there was no doubt that she was dead. But another part of Mullen argued otherwise and so he lowered himself over the woman, laced his hands under her shoulders and dragged at her. Initially she resisted. Mullen tugged harder. Without warning the resistance disappeared and Mullen stumbled backwards. His right foot slipped and for a moment he thought he was going to fall in. Desperately he searched for a purchase and found one. Then, step by cautious step, he reversed himself back along the trunk towards the riverbank, conscious of the woman's weight in his arms. Her hair brushed against his lips. Instinctively he spat and lifted his head higher, twisting around to check his position. Three or four steps later he reached the bank, where he flopped gratefully down onto the baked soil.

The woman flopped down beside him, twisting and landing on her back. That was when Mullen realised his mistake. The woman was a man — a man with long hair but otherwise unquestionably male. His eyes were wide open and they stared accusingly into Mullen's own, as if to ask him why on earth hadn't he come sooner.

Not that sooner would have been much use. Mullen wasn't a pathologist, but he knew enough about death to recognise that the guy hadn't been alive for some hours. Despite the promise of a hot day to come, Mullen shivered. His t-shirt was pretty much soaked through. As he sat there on the bank, he asked himself the obvious question: why on earth (you plonker!) did you do that when he was so obviously, patently, irrefutably dead? Mullen had no answer for himself, beyond a sense that there had been no other option. You don't leave a woman — or indeed a man — face down in the river, even if she is undeniably a corpse. That was Mullen's view, even if it wasn't the police's. Detective Inspector Dorkin informed him of this in the bluntest of terms as soon as he arrived on the scene.

Dorkin was suffering from low blood sugar, Mullen concluded, before very quickly changing his mind. Maybe he was always like this. Certainly the two uniformed officers treated Dorkin with the exaggerated respect people give to self-important celebrities and dangerous dogs. He might as well have had a label in bright red letters stapled on his forehead: 'Highly unstable explosive. Handle with extreme care!'

Dorkin hurled a few direct questions at Mullen — "What time did you find the body? Do you often come jogging here at such an ungodly time in the morning? Did you see anyone else?" — and then lost interest. Mullen, who just wanted to get back to his flat for a hot shower and dry clothes, found himself passing his personal details to the uniformed sergeant, who was altogether more friendly.

"I just need some contact information then you can get home." He ran his eyes up and down Mullen's drenched profile. "I don't suppose you've got any ID on you?"

"It's at home."

"And home is where?"

Mullen gave him his address in Iffley Road. It was only temporary, but he decided not to mention that. It would only complicate matters.

"Your mobile number?"

Mullen told him.

The sergeant wrote it down. Then he punched it into his own mobile. He waited for the one in Mullen's hand to ring. He smiled. "It's so easy to write numbers down wrong."

Mullen smiled back, unconvinced. The guy wanted to check he hadn't given him a dud number. Not that he blamed him. He would have done the same in the circumstances.

"Do you have a work number?"

"I'm self-employed."

Again the sergeant smiled. "And what does 'self-employed' mean in your case?"

"I'm a private investigator."

The smile disappeared. "Really?"

"Yeah," Mullen replied. He felt a jolt of irritation. He thought he preferred the blunt Dorkin after all. "Really."

The sergeant scowled.

"There's no ID on him at all." It was Dorkin, snarling the information out to no-one in particular. He was standing over the body, a black wallet in his hands. "It's been cleaned out. Not a dicky bird."

"Off you go, then," the sergeant said to Mullen. He thrust a card into his hand. "If you think of anything else, give me a bell."

Mullen nodded and turned away. For the briefest of moments, he had been tempted to say something more, but neither policeman had earned his co-operation. Why should he make their life easier?

* * *

Mullen had been calling himself a private detective for less than a month. It wasn't something he felt called to. It wasn't even something he had particularly wanted to do. It was essentially the result of desperation and chance. The desperation had grown like a cancer for several weeks, at precisely the same rate as the money in his bank account had shrunk. As for chance, that had been a conversation overheard in a coffee shop on the Cowley Road. It had been pouring down outside and Mullen had been seeing how long he could eke out a single Americano while he read the free newspaper which he had commandeered from the rack. The conversation had been taking place between two women at the table next to him and the topic had been their husbands. One husband, it appeared, was the model of conjugal loyalty and reliability, his only drawback apparently being a liking for Arnold Schwarzenegger films. His wife was trim and blonde and rather pleased with herself. It was the other woman that Mullen felt rather sorry for. She was the plain Jane of the pair, with a pinched face, large eyes and misery writ large across her features. Her husband, she was telling her friend, was cheating on her. At least, she thought he was. All she needed was proof. And she was pretty darned sure that it wasn't the first time.

"Why don't you hire someone?" the smug friend had suggested. "Catch him in flagrante delicto!" The idea seemed to excite her.

"But suppose he is cheating on me," came the reply. "What do I do then?"

At that intriguing point the fire alarm sounded. Mullen had dutifully exited the café, making sure he took his coffee cup with him. Everyone, it seemed, had assumed it was a false alarm because there was no sign of panic, just as there was no sign of smoke or flames. Out on the pavement he had looked around for the women, eager to continue his eavesdropping, but they had disappeared from view.

Though they were gone, the thought patterns which their conversation had sparked remained behind, like wisps of smoke. So much so that after four cans of cheap lager that evening and a third-rate Bruce Willis film, Mullen had conceded defeat and set about reinventing himself on the internet. This had consisted of setting up a one-page website on which he described himself as 'Doug Mullen, Private Investigator. Discretion assured.' He had ruminated over this for some time, before eventually adding a hostage to fortune: 'Fee payable only if job completed successfully.' It was, he knew instinctively, a daft thing to promise. But anything that gave him an edge seemed worth a try. Besides, he could always turn down anything that wasn't straightforward.

But putting yourself out there on the internet doesn't mean thousands of suspicious spouses are suddenly scanning your website. For a week Mullen waited for something to happen. Nothing did. So he went on-line and ordered himself some business cards. Matt finish one side, blank on the reverse, again offering a 'no win, no fee' service. It was amazing how cheap a thousand cards could be if you ignored all the tempting extras the website tried to entice you into. When they arrived two days later neatly packaged in a box, Mullen felt a brief surge of excitement followed by a lurch of desperation as reality hit home; how on earth, he asked himself, was he going to get rid of them? Pubs, cafes, takeaways, community noticeboards, libraries — there were plenty of places to leave your business cards lying about or pinned up, but it would take a heck of a lot of pavement pounding to distribute them effectively. And how long would they survive before being cleared away by officious proprietors, zealous waiting staff or overworked cleaners? A thousand cards was, frankly, a lot. Nevertheless, Mullen was not a man to throw in the towel, at least not this early in an enterprise. So on the Tuesday he covered East Oxford, on the Wednesday Jericho and North Oxford and on the Thursday Headington. On the Friday morning, with over 500 cards still left and not a single in-coming phone call received, he decided to head to Abingdon. He took the bus, dropping a card on the seat at the front of the bus as he pretended to wrestle with his bus ticket. He took up position half-way back, curious to see the reaction of whoever it was who picked the card up. Almost immediately an overweight man with a red sweating face eased his body onto the seat, oblivious of the invitation beneath his buttocks. Mullen shut his eyes. It was going to be a long day.

* * *

Life, Janice Atkinson had come to realise, was a series of ifs. Not as in Kipling's imperialist poem: 'If you can keep your head when all about you are losing theirs.' That was the level of advice her father had handed out to her on the rare occasions when he had been (a) present and (b) sober, ignoring — or possibly ignorant of — the last line of the poem, which was 'you'll be a man, my son.' Or maybe that was his way of dealing with the disappointment of her being female — pretending that she wasn't.

If!

If she hadn't happened to be in the loo when her mother-in-law rang and therefore had to leave a voice message announcing she would be 'passing by' later that morning and would call in for a coffee.

If she hadn't reacted by catching the first bus out of town, to Abingdon, and deliberately leaving her mobile at home so she couldn't be contacted by her mother-in-law — or indeed anyone else.

If the heavens had not happened to open as she was heading along Ock Street, causing her to duck into the coffee shop she was just passing.

If. If. If.

The man who sat down in the corner was wearing a brown leather jacket. She liked a man in a good leather jacket; and it was a good leather jacket. She could tell that even though he was two tables away and she could see only his back. It was, admittedly, rather worn, but if anything that made him of greater interest to her. She felt a wild urge to walk over and run her hands down his spine, to feel the softness of the leather with her finger tips, not to mention the hardness of the body underneath. But Janice Atkinson wasn't that sort of person, so she remained exactly where she was. His hair was short — a number one cut, unless it was perhaps a shaven head that had, like her own lawn, been allowed to grow untended for too long. His ears protruded somewhat and there was a visible scar across the back of his neck, which made him all the more intriguing. She took all this in via occasional glances over the top of her Daily Telegraph. Eventually the man got up and stretched. He walked over to the notice board near the front door. Janice had herself glanced at it as she stripped off her dripping mackintosh in the doorway. It had contained an eclectic mix of stuff: from plumbers to party planners, an autism support group, two amateur dramatics groups and an invitation to come tea dancing. She lifted the Daily Telegraph higher and turned a page, but her eyes remained on the man in the brown jacket. He pulled a drawing pin out of the board, ferreted in an inside pocket and then stuck a small card up on the board. After that, he zipped up his jacket and walked out.

Janice watched him through the window. She saw him stop on the pavement, looking right and left as if unsure where to go next, before striding off towards the town square. For several seconds she remained unmoving, her lips puckering in thought. Then she stood up and went over to the noticeboard. As she had assumed, he had pinned up a business card. She stared at it for several seconds. Then she unpinned it, returned to her table and slipped it into her handbag.

* * *

Tracking Janice Atkinson's husband had proved a very straightforward first assignment for Mullen. On three separate evenings Mullen had followed Paul Atkinson after work and on each occasion he had obtained remarkably good photos which were, by his reckoning, evidence about as watertight as any wronged wife could possibly wish for. The object of Paul Atkinson's attentions was a surprisingly bulky redhead with a taste for loud floral patterns, a ferociously fruity laugh and an appetite to match. It was clear to Mullen that Atkinson was besotted with her. Even in the public space of the hotel bar where they met each evening, Atkinson was unable to keep his hands off her.

The following Friday Mullen met up with Janice Atkinson in a retro coffee bar on Oxford's Cowley Road. He got there at two twenty, ten minutes early. He was relieved to see it was sparsely occupied, and as he sat at the back, waiting for his Americano to cool, he realised with some alarm that he wasn't looking forward to their meeting one little bit. He ran his hand across his forehead. There were beads of moisture on it. He took off his jacket and wiped his brow. He would be glad to receive his fee — of course he would — but as for giving the wretched woman the bad news and confirming her worst fears, that was something he really wasn't ready for.

When he saw Janice advancing across the floor, he stood up like a nervous young man on a first date. As soon as they were both sitting down, he looked for the waitress but she was already heading their way.

Janice ordered a green tea.

"This is on me," Mullen said, like some big-hearted Harry. And immediately he regretted it. He was preparing her for bad news and she saw it immediately. Her face deflated like a balloon that has developed a leak and he hated himself. He felt a spurt of shame and self-disgust at the job he had chosen to do. But there was no going back. This, he realised, was where he opened Pandora's Box. Whatever came out of the meeting, there would be no going back for Janice Atkinson. And he was going about it with all the tact of a bull elephant on the rampage.

"Well?" She spoke in a whisper, her lips barely moving. She was wearing her hair tucked behind her ears, which accentuated the tightness in her face and the anxiety in her eyes.

Mullen said nothing, conscious that whatever he did say would almost certainly be wrong. Just as wrong as sliding a brown envelope of incriminating photographs across the table. But that was what he did anyway because he had to say or do something.

She turned it over as if examining it for booby traps. There was nothing written on it. It was just a plain brown envelope with stuff inside it. With a sudden flick of her left hand — the third finger, he noticed, was decorated with a seriously expensive diamond ring plus a plain gold wedding band — she ripped it open and slipped its contents onto the table in front of her. Mullen flicked a glance beyond her; she didn't seem bothered about rubberneckers. There were some twenty photographs in the pile — Mullen had, of course, taken a lot more than that, but twenty had seemed to him more than sufficient for their meeting. She began to tap the sides of the pile, until all twenty pieces of evidence were perfectly ordered.

"Here's your green tea." The waitress had appeared by the table and was slowly unloading a small pot, a cup and saucer and a couple of sugar sachets onto the table. "Anything else I can get you?" She hovered longer than was necessary. Mullen's thought so anyway, though Janice Atkinson seemed not to care.

"No thank you."

Janice began to leaf through the photographs. She looked at each one carefully for maybe four or five seconds before moving onto the next. She made no comments. When she got to the end, she slipped them back in the envelope and leant back.

"Job done then."

Mullen nodded.

"I guess I owe you some money."

Mullen nodded again.

Janice Atkinson was studying him intently. "Cat got your tongue?"

Mullen knew he should say something, but the words wouldn't come. He wondered if she was going to burst into tears. He ought to carry a packet of tissues for times like this. It ought to be part of the private eye's standard kit.

But Janice didn't cry. Instead she picked up her cup in her right hand. Her fingers and thumb were tight as pliers around it. For a moment Mullen thought it might shatter in her hand. Or was she going to hurl cup and green tea all over him? After such bad news, he would hardly have blamed her if she did.

Mullen knew he had to say something. "Actually," he said, "It's the first time I've done this."

If he hoped to elicit sympathy, he failed miserably. "I bet you enjoy it, don't you? Poking into other people's secrets and lies?" She leant forward, hissing her fury. "What sort of man are you, Mullen?"

He winced. He felt her pain, but he knew his own too. "Look, I didn't enjoy it. Not one little bit. But I need the money. Anyway, it was you who answered my advertisement."

They glared at each other for several seconds. Then she dropped her gaze, her anger apparently spent. "Sorry." Her voice was a whisper again. She leant forward. An observer might have assumed they were close, even intimate. "It's my first time too." Mullen shifted uneasily in his seat. He wanted to leave, but she hadn't paid him yet.

As if reading his mind, she pulled a smaller envelope out of her bag and held it nonchalantly in her hand.

"What's her name?"

Mullen said nothing. He hadn't intended to tell Janice in case she went round to the woman's house and beat her half to death. He imagined she was more than capable of it.

"What's the name of the bitch that is sleeping with my husband?"

Mullen tried a final, futile defence.

"Does it matter?"

"Name and address." She waved the envelope in the air. "Then, and only then, do I pay you."

He could probably have grabbed it; he could move fast when he needed to. But in the circumstances, in a public place, who knew where that might lead?

"Well?" She pulled the envelope close to her body, alert to all possibilities.

"Becca Baines."

"Address?"

"Wood Farm Road." He gave her the number too. It was a flat half-way up a characterless tower block. He had followed her home one evening.

She didn't bother to write it down. Mary Tudor was said to have had Calais engraved on her heart. Maybe the words 'Becca Baines, Wood Farm Road' were already carved into Janice Atkinson's. Mullen wondered if he had made a big mistake. Suppose she went storming round there and took her revenge?

She gave a thin smile. "Thank you, Mr Mullen." She flipped the envelope across the table. It collided with his half-drunk coffee, but the mug stayed upright.

"Everything all right?"

Startled, they both looked up. It was the waitress again, appearing like the bad fairy. Or the nosy neighbour.

Janice pointedly ignored her. She raised her eyes to Mullen. "Do you think we can get a proper drink somewhere round here?" she said. "It'll be on me."

* * *

Janice Atkinson was wanting more than alcohol. That much seemed clear to Mullen, but mixing work and pleasure seemed (at the very least) unnecessarily complicated, especially when he had been shadowing the woman's husband for the last few days. Besides, he didn't fancy Janice in the slightest. Sure, he felt sorry for her. But that was as far as it went.

She kept giggling. Mullen couldn't keep up. One moment she had been bullying him into submission and the next she was throwing herself at him like a teenage groupie at a rock star. Women were so hard to understand.

Dutifully he laughed at her jokes and reassured her that he couldn't possibly understand why Paul should prefer an overweight bitch like Becca Baines to her. That was a lie, of course. He could definitely see why a man would find Baines very attractive. But in the circumstances a lie seemed preferable.

Mullen let her blether on while he downed his pint as quickly as he decently could. Then he made his excuses.

"I really have got to go," he said. "Work calls."

"Yeah, right."

Mullen felt he had to explain. "I help out at a drop-in on Friday evenings."

"Not snooping on people then?"

He ignored the jibe. "The Meeting Place, down in Cowley. We provide food, friendship and—"

Janice cut in. "All right, off you go then. Mustn't stop you doing your good works."

He stood up and for a moment or three he hovered, just like the waitress at the café.

"Bugger off, then!" She dismissed him with a wave of her hand.

He nodded, turned and headed towards the exit; a naughty schoolboy sent out of the classroom. As he pulled the door open, he half turned. She was watching him. But her face remained impassive as a mask.

Chapter 2

When Mullen arrived at the Meeting Place at 5.30 p.m. on the dot, he immediately sensed that something was different. There were more than the usual number of clients for this time of day and the conversations were muted and secretive. The World Cup had kicked off only the night before and yet no-one seemed to be talking about it. Mullen wasn't much interested in any case. The patriot inside him wanted England to surprise everyone and win the thing — preferably beating Germany in the process — but the realist told him that this was only marginally more likely than the moon turning out to be made of cheese. He made his way through the throng and greeted his fellow volunteers. Kay and Alex were already hard at work making sandwiches, and the manager Kevin Branston, broad of beam and heavily bearded, homed in on him, clapping him unnecessarily hard on the upper arm.

"Good to see you, Doug. Can you mingle tonight?"

Doug had been asked to mingle every session since Branston had discovered he had a military background. "We need someone who can handle himself in a difficult situation," he had explained on that occasion, ignoring the fact that Mullen had just told him his expertise had been in communications, not hand-to-hand combat. Mullen's army career had lasted barely two years, but Branston was now convinced that his usefulness lay primarily in dealing with any nastiness that might suddenly erupt. This became more understandable to Mullen when he looked around at the rest of the volunteers: all of them, with the exception of the stick-thin student Mel, were well past pensionable age.

"See the Brazil game last night?" Mullen asked, keen to make use of the time he had wasted in front of the TV.

Branston ignored the question. "Folks are a bit on edge," he said. "Chris was fished out of the river a couple of days ago."

"Chris?" For the briefest moment, Mullen wondered what on earth Branston was talking about. And then all the bells in his head started ringing in unison.

"Shoulder-length blonde hair tied in a ponytail, camouflage clothes, bare feet and sandals?"

"Of course."

"Two mornings ago. Some jogger fished him out of the water."

Mullen looked hard at Branston. Did he know it was he who had pulled Chris out of the river? Was Branston giving him a prod to see how he would react? He wouldn't have put it past him. But Branston's mind had apparently moved on to other things. His eyes were traversing the room, looking for someone or checking for trouble. "Anyway, keep on your toes, Mullen." He patted him on the shoulder and then he was off. Mullen watched him wend his way through the scrum of people queuing for their food. He didn't warm to Branston. Apart from his patronising manner, there was something shifty about him — a man you couldn't quite pin down or trust. Or was that Mullen's own paranoia kicking in? He shook himself. It was time to concentrate on the clients.

Suddenly another hand — or rather a finger — jabbed Mullen in the shoulder blade. He spun around, hands raised, ready to attack or defend. Old habits die hard.

"Steady up, matey." It was DI Dorkin. "Assaulting an officer can get you in a lot of trouble."

Mullen dropped his hands. "And so can creeping up on people without warning."

"You're a regular here are you?"

"I volunteer every Friday."

"Bit of a coincidence." Dorkin scratched at his neck, and then pulled at the collar of his tieless white shirt. He was, Mullen reckoned, the sort of man who would never look comfortable in a suit even though he wouldn't dream of coming to work without one.

"Is that it?" Mullen asked.

"No," came the reply. "I think we need a little chat."

* * *

The 'little chat' took place in Branston's office, which Dorkin had established as his centre of operations for the evening. Branston had been banished and a seriously young uniformed PC stood in the corner of the room trying to look more important than he was. Mullen sat down on a plastic green chair with a comfort value of zero and waited. Dorkin undid the buttons of his jacket and dumped himself into Branston's office chair. He adjusted its height — up, down and then up again — until he was satisfied. He jiggled from side to side, as if settling himself in for the long haul. Then he unleashed a grin.

"So, Mr Mullen. What have you got to say for yourself?"

Mullen shrugged. As questions went, it didn't exactly demand a reply.

"You see," Dorkin continued, "there's something I don't quite get, Mr Mullen. You come across a dead body in the river. You fish him out. Like a good upright citizen you dial 999. But then, when questioned, you fail to mention the fact that you know him."

During the time Dorkin had been settling himself into Branston's chair, Mullen had been thinking hard about this question. He knew that if Dorkin was an even half-competent detective, he was bound to ask something along these lines. But despite this opportunity to prepare an answer, Mullen doubted that it was going to cut much ice with the laughing policeman here.

"I didn't exactly know him. I've only been coming here for six weeks, on Fridays. Chris was just one of a hundred people thronging the place." He hoped it didn't sound quite as feeble as he feared.

"But you've spoken to him here, right?"

Mullen paused. Was this a fishing expedition? Was Dorkin just casting a line and hoping for a bite?

"Branston definitely thinks you have." The detective sat very still, watching Mullen as if they were playing 'Who blinks first?'

Mullen shrugged. He knew he had to say something. "I've probably spoken to half the people here. In the sense of passing the time of day, apologising that I don't have a spare cigarette, or telling them to tone things down. That doesn't mean I'd recognise them all if I found them floating face-down in the river."

Dorkin's eyes narrowed. "I'd have thought that as a private eye you'd be good at remembering faces."

"I've not been doing it long, have I? Still wearing my L plates." Mullen smiled, trying to laugh off the question, but Dorkin was having none of it.

"Don't get smart with me, Muggins. I could make life very difficult for you."

A warning light flashed somewhere in Mullen's brain. He had once knocked out a squaddie who had teased him about his name. He clenched his hands over his stomach and reined in the impulse to do the same with Dorkin.

"Okay, the fact is I didn't recognise Chris. Maybe you're right. Maybe I should have. But I didn't."

Dorkin leant back in his chair and gave Mullen another of his full frontal grins. He seemed to be pleased with what he had achieved. "As far as I am concerned, Muggins, you can clear off back to work. Just so long as you tell me what it was you and Chris talked about."

Mullen smiled back, now fully under control. He had an answer, a very credible one. "The World Cup," he said.

* * *

Across the other side of the city, at pretty much the same moment as Mullen was checking in for his shift at the Meeting Place, Janice Atkinson was waking up on her sofa. She wasn't used to drinking alcohol in the middle of the day, especially on an empty stomach, and it had made her ridiculously light-headed, and dopey to boot. She was conscious that she had made a bit of a fool of herself with Doug Mullen, so much so that he had downed his pint and exited the pub with indecent haste. She had, briefly, hated him for that. He could at least have bought her a drink. She had paid him enough. As it was, she had had to buy herself a second large glass of white wine and then drink it on her own. She had picked up a newspaper which someone had left on a nearby seat and had tried to concentrate on reading it, but her brain refused to co-operate. A gaunt young man with a body odour problem had sat himself down on the other side of the table without so much as a 'do you mind' and attempted to chat her up. As it happened, she had minded, so she drained what was left in her glass and left, feeling very sorry for herself.

Back home, she had lain down on the sofa and fallen asleep, waking only when the grandfather clock chimed five. She went to the toilet — very necessary — and then checked her mobile in the kitchen. A new text message from Paul informed her that he was going out to play squash later, so only wanted a light meal. She snorted, but set about preparing it anyway. At 5.55 p.m. he arrived home in an upbeat mood. They ate in the kitchen with the TV news on in the background. They exchanged pleasantries and actually agreed that the prospect of four weeks of World Cup football dominating the headlines and the TV schedules was just too much to bear thinking about. Afterwards Paul went upstairs to change and gather together his kit. By seven he had left to meet up with his friend Charles Speight.

Or so he said. Janice wasn't convinced. All this fussing about his gear could have been a pretence. She had never been so gullible as to believe everything that her husband said and recent events had made her even more sceptical. She waited ten minutes while she made herself a coffee — she really did need a clearer head — and then she put in a call to Rachel Speight. Ostensibly this was to ask her if she'd like to meet for lunch the following week, but in reality it was to establish if Charles was indeed playing squash with her husband that evening. He was. Or at least that was clearly what Rachel believed.

Janice double-checked that the front door was locked and slipped the security chain across. The last thing she wanted was for Paul to return unexpectedly. She settled back down at the kitchen table. She had a couple of hours at least to come up with a plan. She laid out several of Mullen's photographs and studied her husband chatting to, laughing with, touching and even kissing the woman. Becca Baines. She had thought at first that Mullen wasn't going to give her the bitch's name. And especially not her address. But he had caved in soon enough when he saw the envelope of money in her hand. He wasn't so tough after all. Show a man you aren't going to take any nonsense and you soon discover what he's made of. Marshmallow in Mullen's case. Presumably he had been worried she might go round to Wood Farm armed with a rolling pin or piece of lead piping and inflict some serious damage on the fat cow.

That was the thing she most resented: the woman with whom her husband was messing about — she tried not to think of them as actually having sexual intercourse — was fat. In fact, she reckoned Becca must, technically speaking, be obese. But that thought made Janice feel even angrier. What had Becca got that she hadn't? Janice downed her coffee, imagining it to be a giant-sized gin and tonic, and swore into the silence of the kitchen. The answer to her unspoken question was simple. What Becca had was youth. It was undeniable. She must be ten years younger, maybe fifteen. But she also wobbled like a jelly. Janice told herself that, unlike Becca the Fat, she had looked after herself diligently over the years: a personal trainer; a boutique hair-dresser in Jericho; daily applications of all sorts of creams to revitalise her skin and put off the inevitable onset of ageing; she had even put herself through seaweed wraps on several occasions. She had avoided Botox. That, as far as she was concerned, was going too far.

Janice focused again on the task in hand and picked up one of the photos from the table. She studied it: Becca's giggling face was close to Paul's, as if telling him a dirty joke or possibly making an obscene suggestion about what they could be doing up in the hotel room Paul had booked. Janice spat at her rival's face and watched with pleasure as a gob of saliva hit her full in the eye. If only she could do that to her in person — or worse! Except that deep down she knew that even if she had the opportunity, she would almost certainly bottle out.

She put the photo back in its place on the table. What was she going to do with them? She ought to have confronted Paul as soon as he got home. She should have laid the photographs out on the table so that he saw them as he walked into the room. Instead she had delivered his supper to him like the perfect Stepford wife and chatted to him about trivialities. What was the point of paying out money to get the photos if she wasn't going to follow it through?

She put her head in her hands and groaned. What on earth was she going to do? Walk out on him with just her pair of matching suitcases? What good would that do her? He'd probably laugh at her, move Becca in and cancel her monthly allowance. Should she change the locks when he was out at work? But how would she stand legally if she did? Paul and his solicitor Nick Newey were as thick as thieves. She would need to find her own solicitor first and get her advice — her advice because the last thing she was going to do was hire a man to represent her. She selected another photo. In this one Paul and Becca were kissing and his hand was touching her bottom. Janice felt the bitter taste of bile rising in her throat and fought it back down. No, she told herself, I will not be beaten. Not by him. Not when he's the one in the wrong.

She stood up and went through to the small study which in theory they both shared, though Paul preferred to lounge on the sofa while checking his emails and do all his internet stuff in front of the giant TV. She opened the third desk drawer and pulled out a brown envelope. She picked up a rollerball pen in her right hand and wrote — rather slowly since she was left-handed — her husband's name and work address on it. Out of the same drawer she located a first class stamp and stuck it on. She went back to the kitchen and inserted that single photo into the envelope, which she sealed. She returned the rest of the photos to Mullen's envelope and hid them in the utility cupboard behind all the cleaning materials. Paul would never find them there. Then she made her way to the front door. There was a mail box at the end of the road and five minutes later the envelope addressed to Paul Atkinson was safely inside it and she was back home.

She went to the fridge, extricated a bottle of white wine — there was always a bottle of white wine chilling in

Janice's fridge — and poured herself a large glass. She would probably regret it later, but she didn't care. She deserved it. The die was cast. She had crossed the Rubicon. She imagined Paul at work on Monday, opening the envelope, his jaw dropping when he realised what the contents were, his Adam's apple bobbing crazily in his throat. Or suppose it wasn't him who opened his post? She had a sudden ghastly thought. Suppose the dragon lady Doreen opened his post for him? Perhaps she should have written 'confidential' on the envelope? What would Doreen say or think? She tried to picture the moment as Doreen, all pursed lips and tasteless fashion sense, handed over the offending article to Paul, thumb and forefinger holding it by the corner as if she might infect herself.

Then Janice began to laugh hysterically. It was a great picture.

* * *

Mullen staggered down the seven steps to the pavement and heaved the box unceremoniously into the boot. This one contained a significant part of his worldly goods, though few of them had any financial or emotional value. A small selection of cutlery, three tasteless mugs, two saucepans, a tray, a small LED desk lamp, a tin decorated with a Dickensian Christmas scene (and containing just four tea bags), cling film, refuse bags and so on. The rear section of his tired old Peugeot was already jam-packed with two cases, two other boxes and several plastic bags. He believed in minimal possessions, and it was ridiculous how much clobber he had collected since his return to the UK. There were a few more bags still waiting to be shifted out of his miserable flat, but that would then be that.

"Excuse me."

Mullen turned and found himself faced by a woman.

Cute! That was his first thought, though he wasn't stupid enough to say so. She had dark curly hair, a round face, a single mole on her right cheek and grey-green eyes that looked right into his — and maybe beyond. She was, he reckoned, about thirty. Maybe this was his lucky day.

"Are you Doug Mullen?"

"I am."

"This Doug Mullen?" She held up one of his business cards.

He nodded. He was wondering how she knew to find him here when his card carried only a website, email address and mobile number.

"Janice recommended you," she said, still giving him the deep-stare treatment. Janice. Whom he had last seen in the Cricketers Arms, misery personified, with the photos of her husband in one hand and an empty glass in the other. To whom he had made his excuses and left for a pressing job that wasn't pressing at all. In point of fact, there hadn't been any job, pressing or otherwise, since then, but Mullen was barely admitting that to himself, let alone to the woman who stood in front of him, appraising him. He wondered how many marks out of ten she was giving him.

"I'm Rose Wilby." She held out her hand. Mullen took it, holding on for slightly longer than was necessary. She glanced at the car. "Are you doing a runner?"

"Moving house."

"So you're not doing a bunk before some unhappy husband comes to get you?"

Mullen gave his default shrug. "Somewhere cheaper — and larger."

"Larger? It can't be Oxford then. Where on earth is it? Outer Mongolia?"

"Boars Hill." Mullen watched her eyes widen. Was it surprise or disbelief? Or both? Not that it was a big deal what she thought, he told himself. But not for the first time in his messy life Mullen was telling himself one thing and believing another. The truth was that attractive women never accosted him in the street, and he wanted it to last for a bit longer. "I'm house-sitting," he said. "For a professor."

Rose gave a curious smile, one side of her mouth slightly higher than the other, as she assessed his excuse-cum-explanation for the fact that he was moving to Oxford's poshest postcode.

"It's ridiculous really. He pays me to live in his large house while he takes a sabbatical with his wife in the States. Mind you, there's a lot of garden to look after and some DIY he wants me to do as part of the deal, but frankly . . ."

She smiled again, this time as if genuinely amused. Mullen dribbled to a halt.

"Any nice wardrobes to explore?"

Mullen was puzzled. Was she flirting?

"C S Lewis? Narnia?"

Mullen could see he had disappointed her. He was suddenly back at school, standing up in front of the class, having failed some critical test.

Rose persisted. "The Lion, the Witch and the Wardrobe. It's a book. The house is owned by a professor."

He finally got the reference. "I've seen the film." He had watched it on TV with his niece Florence. He had rather liked it, except for the bit where Father Christmas appeared. That had seemed odd to him.

Mullen could see that having watched the film was clearly not, as far as Rose Wilby was concerned, in the same league as having read the book. "It's my favourite book ever," she said. There was a pause as each of them considered the chasm that lay between them. "I know!" Her earnest face brightened. "I'll lend you my copy, as long as you promise to return it. Everyone should read it."

"Thank you." He didn't know what else he could say.

"It will appeal to the child in you."

"What makes you think there is a child in me?" He grinned. This was him flirting back.

But it didn't have the desired effect. The crooked smile on her face faded into invisibility. "You're a man, aren't you? And so by definition you're a little boy at heart."

"If you say so."

"Oh I do."

They stood facing each other for several seconds, this time in an enforced conversational silence as an ambulance tore past, siren blaring.

"I'd ask you in for a coffee," he said trying to put things right, "but it's all packed and I really need to get this car moved before the traffic warden comes calling."

"I need to talk to you about a job."

"Your husband, is it?"

She laughed. She held up her left hand, showing him her fingers. Not a ring in sight. "What sort of private investigator are you?"

* * *

Professor Thompson's house was all you might expect of Boars Hill — and more. A sweeping gravel entrance and an honour guard of trees accompanied visitors — in this case Doug Mullen and Rose Wilby — right up to an imposing Edwardian edifice. Rose ran a curious eye over the façade. She looked up to the third storey, where large latticed windows peered out from under the steeply pitched roofs. It was easy to imagine that there might be a wardrobe inside which offered a secret entrance to another world. Not that C.S. Lewis had lived in Boars Hill. She knew that because she had visited his house in Risinghurst. Lewis's home was an altogether much less imposing structure than this one. In some ways she had found it rather disappointing, not least because so much of the original three acres of garden had long since been sold off for development.

"Do you mind if I have a snoop around?" she asked as soon as he had unlocked the oak front door.

She didn't wait for his answer, heading straight up the stairs to the bedrooms, where she took in each room like an estate agent assessing a house for a quick valuation. Downstairs again, as Mullen began to bring his boxes and bags in, she admired the sitting room, the dining room, another sitting room and finally the spacious kitchen with walk-in larder.

The professor — or rather, she suspected, the professor's wife — had left a considerable supply of tinned and dry goods in the larder. She wondered if Mullen was free to raid their supplies as he liked. Returning to the kitchen, she filled and switched on the kettle, located tea bags and mugs and found a fresh pint of milk sitting unopened in the fridge.

Two minutes later they were sitting down in the kitchen at either end of a long oak table.

"Janice was full of praise for you," she said. It wasn't entirely true. Janice had said he was very good at tracking her husband, though she had only admitted this after she had got her to promise on the Bible not to reveal this to anyone. But Janice had been much less complimentary about other aspects of Mullen. "Morally unreliable if you ask me," had been one of her comments. And, "I bet he looks at himself in the mirror every morning." Which had only caused Rose to wonder whether Janice had made a pass at him and been rebuffed.

"This is a slightly different job from tracking an errant husband," she continued. "I want you to find out what happened to a friend of mine called Chris." Her grey-green eyes saw his blue ones blink in surprise.

"They found him floating face down in the River Thames. Bloodstream full of alcohol. Fell in drunk and drowned." She paused again, wondering if Mullen would admit to knowing Chris. This was a test. Pass or fail. Right or wrong.

"It was me who found him," Mullen said. He had passed.

"I know."

"Who told you?"

She nearly said. It wouldn't matter if he knew. But she didn't want to spoon feed the man. Make him work for it.

She unzipped her handbag, removed a small white envelope and placed it on the table. "£300 to show my goodwill. Or rather our goodwill. It's a group effort."

Mullen didn't even pick up the envelope. That was a plus mark as far as she was concerned. Instead he said, "You haven't exactly given me a lot to go on."

"I only knew Chris after he started coming to our church a couple of months ago. Sunday mornings and Thursday lunchtimes. I liked him. Lots of us did. Good with the old. Good with the young. He rubbed some people in St Mark's up the wrong way, but I liked him."

She shivered. It was colder in the house than it was outside. She wished she'd brought a cardigan or jacket.

Mullen rose from his chair. He ran his fingers through what little hair hadn't been removed by the barber. "So you think his death is suspicious?"

She nodded, though in her head she was saying 'stupid question.' Of course she did. Why would she be here otherwise? "Chris didn't drink," she said. "He told me he'd been on the wagon for three years. I believed him." She fixed Mullen with her eyes.

"Why don't you tell the police all this?"

"I have. But they've already come to the conclusion that he relapsed, got drunk and fell in. Pure and simple. A detective came round to the church this morning. Detective Inspector Dorkin according to his ID. Said they weren't likely to spend too much time on an open-and-shut case like this."

Mullen, who had moved across to the sink, twisted his head round and nodded. She got the sense that he was getting interested finally, but not (curiously) so much in the envelope of cash on the table or indeed in her — though he had run an appraising pair of eyes up and down her in the Iffley Road — but in Chris. She wondered why.

"Chris is a nobody as far as they are concerned," she continued. "Why waste valuable police resources on a nobody?"

Mullen nodded again, like one of those ridiculous dogs that drivers sometimes put in the back window of their cars. She looked at her watch. "So are you taking the case, or what?" It was time for Mullen to make a decision.

He opened his mouth, but said nothing. She could see the uncertainty in his face. Was he thinking of a polite way to say 'No'?

"I appreciate it's a long shot," she said, "so my colleagues and I will not expect you to hand back the £300 if you fail in your assignment."

"That's kind."

"Is that a 'yes' or a 'no'?"

"Yes."

"In that case, I suggest you come to church tomorrow and meet people who knew Chris. I've written the details on the back of the envelope."

With that, Rose Wilby hoisted her bag over her shoulder and made her exit.

Chapter 3

Mullen didn't hate churches. That was too strong a word. He merely disliked them. Cornered at a party and asked for his reasons he would very likely have trotted out the words 'irrelevance' and 'hypocrisy.' If pressed further and the drink had been talking, he might well have embarked on a diatribe about the dangers of all types of extreme religious belief. When you've seen people blown up by a suicide bomber, all in the name of someone's God, it's impossible not to have strong feelings.

He was sitting in a pew in St Mark's next to Rose Wilby. It was, by his reckoning, thirty seconds after the official start time of the ten-thirty service, but the vicar — low key in blue clerical blouse and collar, plus darker blue skirt with matching sandals — was showing no sign of getting things started. Glancing behind him Mullen saw punters still drifting in. He turned back. Rose was whispering to her other neighbour, a middle-aged man with a goatee and glasses. Two old ladies sitting at the front had turned round and were looking at Mullen as if he was the major attraction in a zoo. He stared back and they turned quickly away. Mullen tried not to mind. Everyone seemed to be wanting to get a look at him. Was that because he was new or because word had got round about who he was? He turned his own gaze back to the vicar and, as if reading his mind, she stood up. Mullen checked his watch. It was what his RSM at the training barracks would have called relaxed time-keeping. Whatever else St Mark's was, it hardly emanated vibes of wild fundamentalism.

Mullen wasn't sure what to make of the service. Several hymns or songs that he didn't recognise, a sermon that involved overhead images and three main points, some intercessions from a man in a wheelchair (including a reference to the death of Chris — no surname provided), all polished off with a blessing from the vicar and an invitation to stay for coffee and tea. So far, so pleasant and harmless.

Rose leant close to him as the congregation sat down and the vicar made her way towards the back of the church. "I'll introduce you to one or two people, but feel free to mingle and ask about Chris." Mullen didn't know a thing about perfumes, but he liked Rose's smell. He wondered momentarily about the etiquette of saying so in church, but by the time he had come to a decision she had risen to her feet and was waving at a woman dressed in bright purple.

Mullen decided he might as well go and get himself a coffee and mingle. He joined the queue at the back of the church. He felt the tap of a hand on his upper arm and turned.

"I don't think we've met," the woman said. Which was a lie, of course, because they had done so on two separate occasions. "My name is Janice and I think you must be Rose's private investigator. Mr Mullen, isn't it?"

He nodded.

She held two coffees and offered him one of them.

"So nice to meet you."

Her left hand pressed against his elbow as she eased him away from the crowd and into the south aisle. He moved compliantly enough, though he was trying to recall the Christian teachings on praising and praying to God one minute and lying through your teeth the next.

"And so glad you have taken on Chris's case."

Janice had been talking loudly, establishing her innocence with a will. Now she turned the volume down to little more than a whisper. "A few of us in St Mark's have clubbed together, so I hope you're going to give us good value for money."

Mullen glanced around. A hexagonal column separated them from the rest of the congregation, allowing them a surprising degree of privacy considering the number of people milling around.

"And why exactly would a few of you good people of St Mark's be so interested in Chris?" If Janice was going to speak her mind, then so would he. "And why indeed are you willing to spend money on me when the police will be running a case file on his death? The coroner will expect a detailed report from them."

"A report that says an unknown down-and-out got drunk, fell into the river and drowned. No sign of foul play. Death by misadventure. Next case please."

"I'm not convinced." And he wasn't. Not convinced that there was anything suspicious to uncover, not convinced as to the motivation of the do-gooders of St Mark's, not convinced about anything except the £300 that he still had safely tucked away inside his wallet.

"Darling!" It was a man's voice. Mullen turned. He recognised both the voice and the face. Not that he had ever spoken to the guy or even met him, except via the lens of a camera. It was Paul Atkinson.

"This is Mr Mullen, Rose's private detective."

She made him sound like a favoured pet.

"Pleased to meet you." Paul Atkinson thrust out a hand. "Found any clues yet, then? Plenty of dodgy characters here if you ask me." He laughed.

Mullen wasn't asking. Merely observing and wondering. Wondering, for instance, if Paul Atkinson was putting on an act just as much as his wife had been a few moments earlier? What did he know? Had she confronted him with the photos? Or had she stored them away as insurance for the future? If the former, did Paul Atkinson know that it was he, Mullen, who had taken them?

"If you're looking for sinners, what better place to start than a church?" Atkinson was clearly the sort of man who didn't merely make a point. He battered it half to death. "Christians are obsessed with sin. 'We have all sinned and fall short of the glory of God,' wrote St Paul. And don't we get reminded of it every Sunday."

"Paul!" Janice hissed. "That's a gross caricature."

There was another laugh and a tossing of the head. "Nice to meet you, Mulligatawny," he said. "Things to do and places to go." And then he was gone, off to irritate some other sap.

In another place and in other circumstances, Mullen would have succumbed to his instinctive desire to knock the man's block off. It had been Dorkin the other day, hiding behind his detective's badge, and now it was Paul Atkinson hiding behind the church and the fact that there were a hundred pious witnesses who would back him up. Mullen clenched his left hand into a fist and thumped himself on the thigh. It was the only way he could express his frustration. He wasn't a man who had grown up learning to turn the other cheek and let prats get off scot free.

Janice didn't follow her husband. She did, however, emit a noise like a frustrated parakeet. She moved half a step forward. "Par for the course I'm afraid, Doug," she whispered. "God only knows why I don't throw him out." She looked at him in appeal. "I could do now, couldn't I?" She reached across, her hand gripping his upper arm for two or three seconds.

Mullen flinched. He felt like he had stepped out of the shallows straight into deep water, his feet suddenly unable to touch the bottom. He took a slug of coffee while he tried to think of something appropriate to say. Whatever he had thought spying on people's spouses might lead to, this sort of emotional complication wasn't one of them.

"Look, Janice," he said, trying to extricate himself without being too brutal. "I need your help. I need to know who in the church knew Chris."

"We all did, pretty much." She paused. "Not biblically of course." She laughed. "But Chris was one of those people you couldn't not notice. His ponytail, his insistence on wearing camouflage clothes, dare I mention his smell — not exactly a typical member of St Mark's."

Mullen tried another angle. "So who in the church is funding me?"

"I am, for one. After all, you were my idea." She rolled her eyes. She was flirting again.

"Jesus!" Mullen said, and then realised his faux pas.

Janice grinned. "Naughty, naughty!"

Mullen drained his coffee. He had had enough messing around. "You're not exactly helping here, Janice."

He turned to move away, but this time her hand touched his shoulder. "Sorry, Doug," she said, suddenly serious. "Just follow me. I'll introduce you to Derek Stanley."

Derek Stanley was the guy with the goatee to whom Rose had failed to introduce him. Nattily dressed in electric blue chinos, pale yellow shirt and stone-coloured linen jacket, he peered at Mullen over his glasses. Janice made the introductions and then withdrew, removing Mullen's coffee mug from his hand as she did so. He felt her nail scratch the inside of his wrist and then she was gone, leaving behind both the smell of her perfume and a host of confused thoughts.

Stanley plunged straight in. "Chris was a nice chap. Chatty, easy-going and helpful. Sorted out the disabled loo when it got blocked one Thursday. He'll be missed."

"Do you remember when he first came to the church?"

"Oh, yes. That's an easy one. Good Friday. Of course we had a service that day, 10.30 start like today, but very different in tone: quiet and reflective. Actually I didn't notice him until the end. That was because he was sitting at the back of the church. My first thoughts were, I fear, rather unchristian." He frowned as if not quite sure how to express his feelings. "I found his camouflage clothes rather . . ." He took off his glasses and allowed them to hang from his neck on their chain. He rubbed at his eyes. They were moist. "Sorry. Perhaps I should explain. My sister Sarah moved to Hungerford in July 1987. A lovely little Berkshire town — or so she thought. Six weeks later Michael Ryan ran amok there and killed fourteen people before shooting himself. Perhaps you remember it? The first person he killed was a mother he came across in Savernake Forest. He let the children go, but he shot her in the back. Thirteen times. "

He fell silent. Mullen waited, conscious Stanley was nowhere near finished.

"Sarah was at home that day. She was sitting in her front room when Ryan passed by, oblivious of everything that was going on outside. Ryan fired four shots through the windows. One of the bullets grazed her temple. She recovered physically, but not emotionally or mentally. One year later to the day, she hanged herself."

There was another long pause. For the second time Mullen felt he wasn't just in deep water, but was in danger of drowning in it. He knew he had to say something. "I'm sorry to have brought it all up again."

Stanley shrugged. "Not your fault. But I suppose the first time I saw Chris standing there at the back of the church, I thought he was Michael Ryan reincarnated. A ghost." He fell silent, and then a half-smile spread across his face. "Don't tell the vicar. She might give me a theological telling off." He leant forward and gripped Mullen's forearm. Mullen tried not to wince. Was this grabbing of arms and patting of shoulders something that all the members of St Mark's did when they got intense and serious?

Stanley, as if sensing his discomfort, released him. "Actually, it has been very good to talk about it. Therapeutic I guess. Not that I'm into stuff like that, but . . ." He shrugged, unable to finish saying whatever it was that he was thinking. A child dressed as an angel danced past and for a moment or two both of them were distracted by the girl.

"But the reality was that Chris was altogether different. Cheerful, sociable, chatty. Not at all like your average mass murderer."

Mullen took the opportunity to move the conversation on. "So when did you last see him?"

"On the Sunday before his death. He came to the morning service and then stayed for the bring-and-share meal. Not that he would have brought any food, I dare say. But that didn't matter. I remember he helped put away the tables at the end."

"What else can you tell me about Chris?"

Stanley seemed surprised by the question. His eyes, unprotected by his glasses, blinked — a mole emerging from darkness. "Not a lot, I suppose. We passed the time of day most Sundays, but how much do you get to know someone from a few chats in church?"

Mullen considered this. It seemed very reasonable. Friendly, but hardly a deep relationship. If so, then why was Stanley one of those paying for him to make a private investigation? Was this an example of Stanley's 'Christian charity'? Or, the cynic inside Mullen said, was this more to do with good old-fashioned guilt that they had somehow failed Chris? Mullen had no immediate answers, but he didn't mind.

He tried another angle. "Do you know where Chris lived?"

Stanley shook his head. "I'm ashamed to say I never asked him. I assumed he had a tent somewhere. There's quite a few people that do that round here, pitch camp somewhere along the river near where the railway crosses it. Especially at this time of the year."

"Did he ever talk about family, where he grew up, jobs he'd done?"

Again there was a shake of the head.

Over Stanley's shoulder Mullen noticed Rose making her way through a scrum of small children who had materialised from somewhere in the parish centre. He took it as a sign and pulled a business card out of his wallet. "In case you think of anything else," he said, handing it to Stanley.

* * *

"How is it all going?" Rose engulfed him with her smile. "Not too much of an ordeal, I hope?"

Mullen wasn't sure if she was referring to Derek Stanley in particular or the whole experience of coming to church.

"Your Chris seems to be a bit of a blank canvas," he said. "Mr Stanley claims to have spoken to him several times, yet he can't really tell me anything substantial, not even where he lived."

Rose frowned as she considered this. The corners of her mouth puckered. Mullen found this absurdly distracting. She was wearing a summer jersey dress, white with yellow and blue flowers, a navy blue linen jacket and a silver chain with a cross round her neck, altogether smarter than when they had met the previous day. He wondered if she had plans for lunch. He wondered too how much — or how little — she knew about Chris. "Do you know where he lived?"

She shook her head. "I assumed he was homeless. In this good weather, a lot of down and outs choose to sleep rough. Or there's O'Hanlon House in Luther Street."

Mullen felt a flash of anger from somewhere deep within him. This wasn't just because of her dismissal of Chris and others like him as 'down and outs,' though he did hate the expression. It was a neat way of consigning people, real flesh and blood people, to a place where they could be forgotten. You could humour them, feed them with a sandwich and a cup of tea, and then ignore the rest of their lives. He had known someone like Chris once, a man named Bill. He had bumped into him near Kings Cross when, aged fifteen, he had decided to leave the misery of home for the bright lights of London. Bill had looked after him and after a while persuaded him to get on a train back home. Bill had been a 'down and out' and Bill had saved his life.

"So you didn't ask Chris where he lived either?" He heard the sharpness in his own voice and, as he saw her face crumple, he immediately regretted it. She looked down, as if studying the stained church carpet, then raised her eyes until they met his. "I thought," she said, "it was kinder not to ask."

There were still seventy or eighty adults and children filling the church with chatter and laughter and (in one case) tears, but the silence that now fell between Mullen and Rose was as thick and unremitting as the Berlin wall in the Cold War days.

"Perhaps it was," Mullen said, trying to undo the damage he had done. In vain.

"My mother has invited you for lunch." A sudden switch of direction.

"Your mother?" he said, trying to ignore the hostility in her voice.

"Surprising though it may seem to you, I have a mother." The temperature between them had plunged way below zero. "Would you like to come or not?"

"I would," he said.

"Come on then." And she turned on her heel, heading for the exit. Mullen followed, conscious that he couldn't have handled things worse if he had tried.

But he didn't make it outside. The Reverend Diana Downey, doing a meet and greet routine by the double doors, stepped forward, hand outstretched. "Mr Mullen, I presume."

"Doug."

"Very nice to have you along today, Doug. I do hope we haven't put you off coming again?" Diana Downey's face crinkled round the edges. Mullen wasn't an expert on perfumes, but she had undoubtedly applied plenty that morning. Her ear-rings were respectively a sun and moon. More New Age than Christian, Mullen thought — though what did he know about either?

"It was a nice service." It was a feeble response; but it wasn't as if he had attended many in his time.

"It was such a shame about Chris," she continued.

Mullen nodded. So she knew why he was here. "Maybe I could talk to you about him?"

"Of course. I don't know how much help I can be, but give me a ring. My number is on the bottom of the service sheet."

"I will."

"Good." Mullen had had his turn. She turned to greet another parishioner who wanted her attention. Mullen took his cue and went outside to catch up with Rose. She was across the other side of the road, talking to Janice and Paul Atkinson. Their heads turned as one towards him and then they broke up, the Atkinsons hurrying off down a path that ran between the houses.

"There you are," Rose said as Mullen reached her. "I thought maybe you had changed your mind."

* * *

Margaret Wilby lived in Grandpont Grange, an elegant stone-faced retirement complex built around a pair of quadrangles in imitation of the archetypical Oxford college. She greeted her daughter rather coolly, Mullen thought, barely allowing herself to be pecked on the cheek. As for him, she nodded curtly and ran her eyes up and down his clothing as if assessing whether he was appropriately dressed for Sunday lunch. Mullen suspected he failed on that score.

"My daughter will offer you a drink," she said, retreating to the kitchen at the end of the large living space they had just entered. Mullen took in the detail. A small dining table (mahogany he guessed) was laid for three. There was a two-seater settee and a pair of matching armchairs grouped around a low oak table. A flat-screen TV stood on a matching oak cabinet in the corner. A tablet device of some sort lay on a side-table (also oak) next to one of the armchairs. The carpet was deep red with a slight fleck.

"There's wine, if you like. We're having red with the lamb," Rose said. "Or my mother has a plentiful supply of dry sherry and gin and tonic."

"Or apple juice or water if you don't drink on duty," her mother said.

Mullen shrugged. "I'm not a policeman. Red wine would be nice."

Margaret Wilby made a guttural noise that might have meant several things, though Mullen doubted if any of them were complimentary. He wondered how soon after they had eaten he could leave without giving offence. It didn't seem to be the happiest mother-daughter relationship and he wasn't sure either of them wanted him there. Which rather begged the question: why had he been asked?

By the time they were sitting down at the table some ten minutes later, Mullen was feeling slightly less jaundiced. He had almost emptied his wine glass and the smell from the food (roast lamb, roast potatoes, vegetables, gravy and mint jelly) was making him realise how hungry he was. He made the faux pas of picking up his knife and fork just as Margaret plunged into a prolonged grace which covered thanks for the food, a request for divine wisdom and regret for the 'passing of poor Chris,' but neither woman appeared to hold it against him. For that he felt truly thankful.

"I would like to make something clear, Mr Mullen." Margaret Wilby spoke as if addressing a meeting of the town council. Mullen was about to lift a forkful of lamb and potato into his mouth. Reluctantly he laid it back on the plate. He paused, waiting for her pronouncement. "I think Rose and her coterie are wasting their money. I cannot see the point of hiring a private detective when the police with all their resources can do a much better job." Mullen looked across at her, but her attention had transferred to her plate: she speared two pieces of carrot and raised them to her mouth. "Well? Haven't you anything to say for yourself?"

"Rose says that Chris did not drink alcohol," Mullen said. "My understanding is that the police pathologist found a high concentration of alcohol in his blood. I see it as my task to investigate this apparent discrepancy."

"I see." Margaret Wilby considered Mullen's answer for several seconds. She took a sip of wine and swilled it round her mouth as if trying to decide if it passed muster. Eventually she swallowed.

Mullen felt he had to say more. "If Chris went on a bender after a period of abstinence, as the police think, then the chances are there will be some evidence somewhere. Someone will have been there at the time, maybe drinking with him. A shop-keeper may remember him buying the booze. Or there might be a stack of empties wherever it was that he slept at night."

"And what happens if you draw a blank? Do you give Rose all the money back? Like it says on your website?"

41

Mullen wondered what Mrs Wilby had done in her earlier life. She would have made a formidable barrister he reckoned.

"If I draw a blank, your daughter has kindly told me she and her colleagues will not be asking for the £300 back."

Margaret Wilby assembled another forkful of food. "In that case, all I can say is you had better make sure you give them good value for their money. Otherwise I shall make life very difficult for you."

Mullen felt a sudden shiver of something close to fear, even though (he told himself) it was ridiculous to be scared of an older lady with pretensions of grandeur and a sharp tongue. But there was no doubting the menace behind her words. Who did she know who could make life difficult for Mullen? Someone high up in the police? The Chief Constable?

"Mother!" Rose said. Her face had turned a deep red and her hands were gripped tightly round her fork and knife, as if she might be about to use them as weapons. "I think it's time we changed the subject."

* * *

When Mullen left Grandpont Grange shortly after three p.m., his only thought was to get back to Boars Hill. Margaret Wilby had eased up on him after her daughter's intervention, but despite the food he had already decided that he would rather eat a flaccid ham sandwich sitting on a park bench than go through that experience again. As far as he was concerned the whole episode had only served to emphasise the truth behind the old adage that there's no such thing as a free lunch. His car was parked in Lincoln Road, beyond the parking restrictions, and he headed straight down the Abingdon Road because that was the quickest (though hardly the most scenic) route. There was another reason too. He stopped at the shop on the corner of Newton Road and bought five packs of ten cigarettes and then continued south, quickening his pace. All he wanted to do was to get 'home,' make a cup of tea and cut the professor's lawn. In peace. Without interruption. On his own.

Chapter 4

O'Hanlon House stands in Luther Street, an easy stone's throw from the magistrates' court and a more vigorous hurl from St Aldate's police station. The main entrance of Christchurch College, centre of academic privilege and touristic pilgrimage, is only a little further up the hill and yet it might as well be in another universe. No tourists ask the way to Luther Street and certainly not to O'Hanlon House, which specialises in providing emergency accommodation for the homeless and help towards permanent resettlement.

Mullen hadn't ever been there himself, but he knew enough about it to know that it would be a good place to start his search. Of course, he could have gone to the Meeting Place and asked questions there, but he didn't want to draw attention to what he was doing and in any case his next shift was four days away. As before, he parked in Lincoln Road to avoid parking restrictions and then walked north along the Abingdon Road. There were places nearer town where he might be able to park for an hour or two if they were not already taken, but he really had no idea how long he would need. Given the speed at which cars and lorries were failing to get into the city centre that Monday morning, he very quickly felt vindicated in his decision — not to mention a little bit smug. Walking was almost as quick and certainly less stressful than driving.

It took him some twenty minutes to reach the bottom of St Aldates. Just past the magistrates' court, he turned left into Speedwell Street, overtaking three motionless buses. Then he turned left again, into Cromwell Street, and saw immediately what he hoped to see. Not O'Hanlon House as such — though of course it stood exactly where it always had, but people. Three men emerged from the front door and ambled slowly towards him. Not that they had noticed him. They seemed instead to be immersed in a deep discussion which involved looking down at an object in the hands of the middle man.

"Hi there, gents!" Mullen called out the greeting from a distance, hoping he sounded cheery and unthreatening. They looked up, surprise and guilt on their faces. "I was hoping you could help me," he said. They had stopped moving forward, but he continued to advance towards them. "I'm looking for someone."

Nobody answered. Mullen slowed to a halt a couple of metres away. The three of them were aligned in height order: the man on the left was at least six feet four by Mullen's reckoning, with a bald head, sunken eyes and a scar along the bottom of the chin parallel to his mouth. He avoided eye contact. The one on the right was the Ronnie Corbett of the three in height, though more of a Ronnie Barker round the waist. Grey hair plastered his head. The man in the middle was similar in height to Mullen, but bulkier and with a leather jacket which suggested he might once have been a Hells Angel.

"Who are you?" the man in the middle asked.

Mullen ignored the question, brandishing instead the photo he had carefully cut out of the newspaper and sealed inside a polythene envelope. He held it out to the middle man.

"We don't talk to the police."

Mullen smiled. "Nor do I! Not if I can help it." He reached inside his jacket pocket, extricated three packets of cigarettes and brandished them.

"His name was Chris," Mullen said. "A friend of a friend wants to know what happened to him and where he dossed down."

"He drowned didn't he?" Ronnie Corbett-Barker was eying the cigarettes with extreme interest. "It was in the papers."

"Did he ever sleep here?" Mullen gestured towards O'Hanlon House.

"Don't think so." The tall guy was joining in now. He didn't want to miss out.

"Are you going to give us a fag or not?" Hells Angel was trying to take charge now. He was evidently the boss in their little group.

"There's a packet each, but not if you lie to me."

"How will you know if we do lie?"

"I'll know where I can find you."

"Is that some sort of threat?"

"I guess it is." Mullen stepped back half a pace and began to put the cigarette packets back in his jacket, all the time keeping his eyes on the ring-leader. He hadn't yet worked out if he was all hot air and wind. He knew from experience how people could explode into violence.

"Last chance," he said. "There are plenty of other people I can ask. Where did Chris sleep at night?"

"Down by the river." It was Ronnie Corbett-Barker again. He held out a hand. "Near where it goes under the railway. There's a whole encampment there."

"No he didn't." Hells Angel stretched out a hand and grabbed his mate by the shoulder. "This dickhead will say anything. Go down the road to Folly Bridge. Then left along the footpath. You'll see all the college boathouses on the left and the university one on the right. Keep walking and after a few hundred yards you'll pass another boathouse. Then it's over a little footbridge and there on the right you'll see bushes. He had a tent there."

Mullen considered what he had heard. Hells Angel sounded convincing, but you never knew. The man held out his hand. "The fags." It was a demand, not a request.

Mullen pulled the three packets out again and handed two of them over. He held up the third in front of them. "One of you is lying, so I'm keeping this one."

Half an hour later Mullen had made his way down the west bank of the river past the college boat houses and over the little humpback footbridge. He found the bushes Hells Angel had talked about and the grassed area beyond, but there was no obvious sign of people or tents or the detritus of life. He spent several minutes checking every possible place where a tent or food or a bag of possessions might have been hidden, but drew a blank. He swore. Hells Angel had well and truly suckered him. The little fat guy must have been telling the truth.

He pulled off his jacket. The sky was pure blue and his shirt was sticky with sweat. He wiped his brow. It was going to be a long hot day.

* * *

At pretty much the same time as Mullen was cursing his own gullibility, Doreen Rankin was dealing with the post addressed to Mr Paul Atkinson of GenMedSoft, a computer software company which specialised in the provision of software for the dental and medical markets. As his personal assistant and office administrator, she took a proprietorial interest in everything that came in addressed to Mr Atkinson personally or to his company generally. She liked to know what was going on, not just because she was nosy, but because her boss regularly failed to keep her informed of important pieces of information which later boomeranged back to hit her with an almighty thwack.

More and more, the interesting and important letters and documents were coming in via email. This was a source of great frustration to Doreen, who now only got to grips with things when Paul Atkinson went on holiday and reluctantly gave her access to his emails. The paper post this morning seemed no different from usual: letters from the Vale of White Horse District Council and from the company who managed the business park, various circulars which went straight into the recycling bin and three A4 envelopes all containing sales brochures. Or so she thought. The first two were indeed that; one she kept just in case and the other she tossed on top of the circulars. Doreen Rankin had a laser-beam eye for detail and she noticed even before she ripped open the third envelope that it was addressed by hand. That in itself was unusual, but not unprecedented. A charity appeal, an over-qualified student looking for paid work or an internship, a local business offering a special catering deal — these were the potential correspondents that flicked through her mind ever so briefly before she ripped the white envelope open. There was no 'Private and Confidential' on it, so it was by her own rules fair enough that she should take charge of it and vet the contents. Paul would almost certainly tell her off for not doing her job if she didn't. He had told her right at the beginning that he didn't want to wade through piles of tedious post when he had more important things to do.

Doreen Rankin, who had been standing up as she prepared to give this final piece of correspondence a thumbs up or down, made a mewing sound and sat down very heavily in her chair. She felt giddy with shock and prurient excitement. Then she stood up, went over and shut the door to her small office, closed the blind on her internal window and returned to the desk. There were three photographs and they all told the same story: Paul Atkinson was having an affair. Not that this came as a surprise to Doreen. She had seen his eyes wander when any young women were within his vicinity and his hands too with a female student who'd come in as a temp. She had been skinny as hell, but the woman in the three photographs was anything but. She needed to go on a crash diet. God only knew what Paul saw in her, but Doreen Rankin had long since given up trying to understand men. She slipped the photographs back into the envelope and slid it into her top drawer, which she locked. She needed time to think. What should she do? Give it to Paul and apologise for having opened it, but commit herself to secrecy? Keep it as insurance against the future? Shred it and pretend she had never received it? Paul had a meeting that morning and wasn't due in the office until after lunch. At least she had some time to think.

* * *

Mullen could have returned the way he had come, up river, but he wanted to buy a bottle of water (why on earth hadn't he brought one with him?). However, there was another good reason for walking over Donnington Bridge, along Weirs Lane and then up the Abingdon Road again (right past where his car was parked). As he saw it, the only way he could find evidence that Chris's death was an accident was to prove to Rose and her church friends that Chris had gone back on the booze. Of course they all wanted to believe he was a reformed character who had forsworn alcohol forever. Mullen understood that. He could sympathise with them for wanting it to be so. But life had hardened him. He held to the view that Chris had most likely relapsed and gone on a bender and had fallen in the river as a result. A pile of empties wherever it was that Chris slept would as good as prove it. Or a friend of Chris prepared to exchange the truth for a couple of packs of cigarettes. Or indeed a shopkeeper who could verify that Chris had bought booze from their shop. Or even a pub. However, pubs were a bit of an endangered species these days. The Wagon and Horses had been turned into a Tesco after considerable local resistance, but Mullen knew that there were two or three others still plying their traditional trade along the road into the city centre, so he would visit them.

If he could find just one piece of evidence of Chris's drinking, that would be quits as far as he was concerned. £300 wasn't a lot for the job, but it would be fair enough in the circumstances. Rose and her friends couldn't complain just because the truth was different from what they wanted it to be.

Mullen made his way steadily up the Abingdon Road, armed with his short spiel and the photograph of Chris. It was an unproductive search: none of the pubs remembered serving him, none of the shops admitted to selling him alcohol, though in two cases they certainly recognised him from the photograph. "He smelt a bit, like they all do," was the first comment. "Came in here from time to time for food or fags, but I can't say I ever had any problems with him."

Mullen nearly challenged the man, but decided there wasn't any point. If that was how the homeless were remembered and judged — whether they were any trouble or not — he couldn't really blame people. But he felt irritated and protective nevertheless. In his experience the homeless could be kind, supportive and loyal, just like anyone else. And if they smelt a bit, was that any surprise?

The woman behind the till in the next shop recognised the photo immediately. "Yes, a very polite man," she said. "Always asked me how I was. Not like most people who are in far too much of a hurry."

"So he was a bit of a regular, was he?"

"Maybe two or three times a week."

"And did he ever buy alcohol?"

Furrows creased her flawless brown skin as she considered the question. "No, not from me. Mind you, I am not on the till all the time."

Mullen found himself warming to her: she didn't want to mislead or pretend certainty if there was any suggestion of doubt — a perfect witness. "Did he ever come into the shop smelling of alcohol?"

She pursed her mouth, but her reply was unequivocal: "No, definitely not."

Mullen picked up a bar of chocolate from the shelves immediately to his right. "I'll have this," he said. It wasn't exactly a chocolate day; the temperature was mid-seventies at least. But he felt he needed to thank her by buying something.

"He had a very nice voice too," she said, handing Mullen his change. "Proper Queen's English."

The encampment which the rotund Ronnie Corbett-Barker had talked about, before being bullied into silence by the Hells Angel, proved to be easy to find. Once Mullen had reached Folly Bridge, he turned left down the footpath and followed the Thames up-river, winding past modern flats and Victorian terraces, college accommodation and sheltered housing and then suddenly there were grass and trees and bushes on his left. Mullen followed the meandering course of the river, passing under a black iron bridge and soon after that beneath the railway. It was then that he saw the settlement, a ragged line of tents stretching away from the main river alongside a meagre tributary.

Mullen paused. He was feeling queasy. He had already devoured the unnecessarily large chocolate bar, conscious that in this heat, it would cause a mess if he didn't. But now he was regretting it. He would have been much better off buying a nice wholemeal sandwich from the delicatessen he had passed. He took a swig of water and advanced. As he got closer, he realised the site was much tidier than he had expected. He imagined most of them either kept their belongings inside their tents or carried them with them. It was also pretty much deserted, excepted for a couple of men sitting together in the shade of a bush. They were playing cards.

When they saw him, they both jumped up.

"What do you want?" one demanded.

"Who are you?" the other added.

Mullen stopped some five metres away from them, conscious of their nervousness and hostility. "Did you know Chris? The guy who drowned in the river, down near Sandford."

"You haven't answered our questions," the first man said. He had a pinched face and a pinched body; his eyes flickered uncertainly on Mullen and on the track to his right, as if weighing up the options of fight or flight. Mullen fiddled in his jacket and located two of the three remaining packets of cigarettes.

"I understand he lived here."

"Do you?" He was giving nothing away. His colleague, shorter and fatter and wearing tartan trousers, was silent, twisting his hands together as if they held a dishcloth that needed wringing out.

"There's a packet of fags each if you just show me which was his tent." He held out his hands but then tucked the cigarettes away back in his pocket.

They both turned and walked further up the tributary, past half a dozen other tents and a couple of bundles. They continued for another thirty-odd metres before they came to a flattened area of grass. A circle of stones around grey ashes showed where a fire had once burned. There was a saucepan, cigarette butts, a filthy red scarf and an empty tin of baked beans. A single mauve sock decorated the ground.

"Didn't he have a tent?" Mullen felt the frustration bubbling up.

"Yeah, sure he did. But someone took it." The man with the pinched face was looking nervous, his eyes searching again for an escape route.

"Don't take the piss, matey. Who took it?" Mullen took a step closer. He wasn't going to be messed about again.

"Some guy."

"What sort of guy?"

"Dunno. I didn't ask him for his name and number. It was early. I wouldn't have seen him except that I needed a pee. He just pulled Chris's tent down and then went through all his stuff. He put most of it in a plastic bag and walked off."

"So he took the tent with him?"

He didn't reply immediately. There was the slightest of pauses. Then: "Yeah."

The other man, who hadn't said a single word, giggled. Mullen looked at him and then back to the pinched one.

Mullen's hand moved like a cobra striking its prey. It grabbed the man by his t-shirt and wrenched him forward until they were eyeball to eyeball. He wasn't giggling now.

"I've already been lied to once today," Mullen snarled. Close up, the man smelt of baked beans and dirt. And fear.

"He's got it." He pointed at the other guy. He licked his lips. His face was greasy with sweat. Mullen held onto his informant, but concentrated his gaze on the other man. He wondered if he was going to try and do a runner.

"Mine had had it," the man said. "Worn out." He spoke quickly and jerkily. "I asked the guy if I could have the tent. He said I could. That was kind of him wasn't it?"

"Show me," Mullen said, releasing his grip.

The tent was a small one, big enough to sleep in and hide from the rain, but not much else. Easy to carry. There wasn't much room to store stuff either, which was probably just as well. There was a sleeping bag piled in a heap in the corner, a full bottle of water and two empty ones, a few clothes under the sleeping bag, a saucepan, a multipack bag of crisps, cans of soup and a couple of toilet rolls. Mullen lay down on the groundsheet and looked up. For a moment he was back in the army on a training course. Three days in some wild bit of Scotland. It had been hot then and it never got properly dark at night. Mullen had liked the outdoors side of the army. As a kid he had loved camping in the small back garden. But living in a tent like this was different. OK in the good weather, but tough when the rain came and the temperatures plunged.

What had Chris thought about as he lay in the tent at night waiting for sleep to come? Had he said his prayers like all the goody-two-shoes folk at St Mark's? Not, of course, that they were all so perfect. Not Paul Atkinson and probably not Janice either.

The problem, Mullen was realising, was that he didn't know much at all about Chris. Did he go to St Mark's to get food and friendship or because he believed in all that Christian stuff? What was it the woman in the shop had said? He spoke proper 'Queen's English.' So he came from a middle or upper class family maybe — a family that would miss him? Surely there was someone who would read the paper and recognise his face? Except that a man dead in the river with a high level of alcohol in him was hardly a story to hit the national papers or go viral on the internet. If his family lived locally, yes. But if they were from some other part of the country, probably not. Or maybe he had no family.

Mullen extricated himself from the tent. The two men were standing together, watching him. A pair of dummies; nervous, fearful even. Mullen began to fiddle in his jacket for the two packets of cigarettes. They had just about earned their reward. Or at least they would do if they gave him a detailed description of the man who had taken away Chris's possessions. It would be a fair exchange. He stretched his right hand out, displaying his peace offerings. "Here," he said.

But they didn't move. They seemed to be holding their breath. It was only then that Mullen realised something was wrong. There was someone behind him. He began to turn, but too late. Something hard smashed into the back of his head. And for Mullen the lights went out.

* * *

"There's something I need to show you."

Paul Atkinson looked up to see Doreen Rankin standing in the doorway, arms folded; a sure sign that there was trouble afoot. He had only just got into the office and was half-way through a sandwich. "In my office," she continued as if she was the boss. "At your convenience." Which of course, as Atkinson knew, she didn't mean.

He nodded and held up his lunch-box to try and buy himself some time, but the pout that formed on her lips and the shrug of her shoulder as she turned away spoke otherwise. Atkinson swore under his breath and stuffed what was left of his ham and pickle sandwich into his mouth. He still had a brie and cranberry one to consume, but he knew better than to delay. It was best to go and see what the bee in her bonnet was and get it sorted out. Then he could eat the rest of his lunch in peace. Life was always more straightforward when Doreen was happy.

"Shut the door," she snapped when he walked into her office.

"This arrived in the post," she said as he sat down. She pushed an envelope across her desk. "I assumed it was the standard marketing bumf, so I opened it as usual."

Atkinson knew there was a problem. Doreen Rankin was getting her excuses in first. She was rarely in the wrong, but when she was the last thing she did was apologise. Instead she came out guns blazing, just as she was doing now. He looked at the envelope: no company stamp; no sender's address; hand-written. He lifted it at an angle and allowed the contents to slide onto the table. They lay there, face up. Atkinson licked his lips, which were suddenly very dry. He picked up and studied the top photograph for several seconds, the others more briefly. He could feel Doreen's eyes boring into his head, but he didn't look up. He needed to think.

"I could shred them of course," Doreen said. She was a problem-solver. That was one of her strengths. Give her a problem and her first reaction was to come up with a solution. But this wasn't her first reaction. She had had plenty of time to think things through. "But whoever sent it will no doubt have the original digital photographs sitting on their computer somewhere ready to be reprinted or emailed round to all and sundry. So the only thing shredding will achieve is to ensure no-one in the office will see these copies by mistake. And possibly pass them on to your wife."

Atkinson looked up at her. She always referred to Janice as his wife and never by her name. Even in the current circumstances, it irritated him. "I can work that out for myself, Doreen."

"Unless, of course . . ." She paused. Atkinson suspected she was rather enjoying this whole embarrassing situation. Even so, another great thing about her was that she was totally loyal. "Unless, of course, your anonymous correspondent has already posted copies of the photographs to her."

Atkinson could feel the blood drain from his face. That was something that hadn't occurred to him. He looked into Doreen's impassive face for some flicker of encouragement.

"Actually, I think that is highly unlikely," she said. "After all, the obvious reason for sending these incriminating photographs to you is in order to blackmail you. And in such circumstances, sending photographs to your wife would be counterproductive."

Atkinson nodded. She was right. She had to be.

"There is another alternative of course," she said.

Paul Atkinson's irritation level went up another notch. Why did Doreen insist on peppering her conversation with words like 'of course'? But he tried not to let his feelings show, because that would only encourage her. Instead he folded his hands together and waited for her to say whatever it was that was so self-evident. He needed her on his side. And if she had a solution to the problem, he would like to hear it.

"Have you given your wife any reason to doubt your fidelity?" She paused momentarily as if she expected him to answer her question. But then she pushed on. "Because it occurs to me that if you have, then she might herself have hired some man to photograph you in the act as it were. In which case her posting them to you at the office where they might get seen by me is her way of applying pressure on you — of yanking on your lead and forcing you to come to heel."

Atkinson considered this. He didn't like the metaphor of himself as a dog and Janice his owner, but he had to admit Doreen had covered all the possibilities. So where on earth did that leave him?

"My advice," Doreen said firmly, in a tone of voice that indicated he had better jolly well take it, "is to allow me to shred the photographs now, and then for you to go home at the usual time and see what happens."

Atkinson opened his mouth. "But—" He got no further.

"It will be obvious from your wife's behaviour whether she knows about the photographs. If she has been sent copies in the post, she will be furious with you as soon as you walk through the door. If it is she who sent them to you, she will no doubt be studying you very carefully. On the other hand, if she knows nothing about it, then her behaviour will be quite normal. In which case you will need to prepare yourself for a phone call or some other communication from your blackmailer."

"Yes." Paul Atkinson could think of no other reply.

"Well," she said, "you can go and eat the rest of your lunch in peace. I'll deal with these photographs and then I'll bring you a coffee." He had been dismissed, and not for the first time, by his personal assistant. But for once he didn't really mind.

* * *

Mullen had no idea where he was. He tried opening his eyes, but shut them instantly as pain jagged through his head.

"Hello there."

He opened his eyes a chink and glimpsed an angel in blue standing over him. She was, he realised, holding his wrist and checking her watch.

"You'll live," she said and laid his arm down. "Are you in pain?"

He nodded, shutting his eyes against the sunlight that was flooding into the room from behind her.

"I'll give you something for it."

He took the analgesics she produced, shut his eyes again and fell asleep. When he next opened them, his angel in blue — her name was Kaila according to her badge — offered him some toast. "You've missed supper," she said. "But we don't want you fading away." She had a nice smile and an ethnicity he couldn't place. Not that her ethnicity mattered, but he was curious nevertheless. "You missed a visitor too. I sent him away." Mullen was grateful. He couldn't think of any 'him' that he would want to be visited by. Maybe it was Dorkin. He seemed to turn up everywhere.

Mullen slept through the night. "Like a baby," he said to Raheema when she asked the next morning. Raheema had replaced Kaila. Mullen was feeling much better, with just a dull throb at the back of his head. He thought he should try and be a bit chatty. 'Like a baby' seemed a good way of doing so.

Raheema looked at him as if he was deranged. "I presume you've never had a baby?"

He shook his head.

"They don't sleep — not more than a few hours."

"It's a saying."

"It's the stupidest saying I've ever heard."

He fell silent. It was evidently a sore subject. Or was she always like this?

"Is there someone we can contact for you?" The storm had passed. "The doctor will be doing his rounds a bit later and if he is happy, we will discharge you. We would prefer it if someone drove you home. Or we can order a taxi."

Mullen tried to think. Only two names came to mind. "Rose Wilby."

"Girlfriend?"

"No," he said quickly, irritated by the nurse's prying.

"Would you like me to ring her for you?"

"Please." Mullen leant back into his pillows. He really would have preferred to stay in hospital for another day or so. He could sleep lots and have nurses waiting on his every need. Maybe Kaila would be back on shift again later. That would be nice. Or maybe Raheema would be replaced by Raheema Mark 2. That would be less nice. He closed his eyes.

When he opened them, time had passed and the figure in front of him was male. The doctor was ridiculously young and wore a stethoscope slung round his neck as if to prove his status in case anyone should mistake him for a schoolboy on work experience.

"That's a nasty blow you got there, Mr Mullen."

"Yeah."

"Luckily you've got a very tough skull."

Mullen said nothing. Was that the culmination of years of expensive training? God help the patients if it was. Or perhaps the man really was a schoolboy on work experience, and masquerading as a doctor.

"As far as we are concerned, you can go home."

"Thanks, Doc."

The doctor-schoolboy sniffed. "Maybe after you've taken a shower."

It wasn't the subtlest of hints, but Mullen wasn't bothered.

He lay there a bit longer, reluctant to do anything. Someone in a green uniform appeared with a trolley. His name was Rick. It said so on his badge. He chatted so volubly that Mullen decided maybe he would like to get home after all.

"Will you be wanting lunch?" Rick asked, ever helpful.

"Not if my lift turns up first."

Rick moved on. Mullen, who had opted for a cup of tea, drank it slowly. Then he went in search of the shower room.

* * *

Becca Baines had only been in the hospital car park ten minutes when Mullen appeared out of the main entrance escorted by a man and a woman. She didn't know either of them. The guy was wearing bright orange-brown chinos and a summer jacket, and the woman was neat and precise in both clothing and movements. Even the dark curls of her hair seemed well controlled. Baines walked slowly towards her own car, a red Fiat Punto, trying to keep an eye on the trio as they made their way across to a blue Vauxhall Astra. Suppose Mullen looked over, saw her and recognised her? But surely he wouldn't. She was wearing sunglasses, a long black wig and a retro dress from the back of the wardrobe which she wouldn't normally be seen dead in. Wasn't that enough of a disguise? She had bought the wig for a fancy dress party, as a bit of a laugh, but it hadn't been that cheap and she had rather liked the effect it had had on a guy called Steve — rock hard biceps and an eagle tattoo on his neck. But Becca needn't have worried about being recognised. Mullen was fully preoccupied by the task of getting to the car. His two escorts were walking so closely he might have been handcuffed to them. The man got into the driver's seat while the woman held open the rear door for Mullen as if he was incapable of doing anything for himself. Mind you, he did have an impressive bandage round his head. The woman bent over him, fussing. Finally, she shut his door and walked round to the other side of the car. She opened the rear door. She was going to sit next to him. Baines puckered her lips, much as Frankie Howard used to do. "Ooh!" Becca could read the body language even at this distance: the woman fancied Mullen.

Becca wanted to laugh out loud, but the Astra was already moving off. She hurriedly squeezed herself into the Punto — no easy task given how close the neighbouring SUV had parked — rammed the key into the ignition and started the engine. By the time she had reached the exit barrier, the Astra was out of sight. There was only one road out, but when she got to the end of it and encountered the junction, she felt the first stirrings of panic. Left or right? A glance each way gave no clues. Logic told her that the chances were they would have turned right. A driver behind her hooted. She shouted abuse into the mirror and followed her instincts, turning right down the hill. There was a blue Mini some distance in front. And a car in front of it. They were slowing down, as red lights gave Baines the chance to close the gap, but seconds later the lights changed and they were on the move again, over a mini roundabout and then right, blue Astra followed by the Mini. She pressed on after them, out to the ring road and then over it before looping back and off towards the Headington roundabout, tucking herself in behind the Mini. She grinned and gave a whoop of joy. This tailing lark wasn't so difficult after all.

The Mini eventually parted company at the Heyford Hill roundabout, heading into Sainsbury's, but the Astra remained on the ring road. Baines kept her distance, happily allowing a white van to slip across in front of her. There was no way Mullen and his two buddies were going to notice they were being followed. She kept them within sight all the way round the ring road, over the A34 and up towards Boars Hill, turning right at the top into Foxcombe Road. She had driven along it often enough. There was a pub further along, unimaginatively called the Fox. Even so, it was a nice place. She had eaten and drunk there several times with a friend and would-be lover. He was water under the bridge now. And good riddance too.

But the Astra wasn't going to the pub. Its tail lights showed red as it braked sharply. Its left-hand indicator flashed orange and immediately the car swung left off the road, bouncing and slightly out of control. Baines braked too, but not so sharply, easing off the accelerator and peering after them. She saw the rear of the car, red lights flickering on and off, and then she was past the entrance. Through the rather feeble cover of the beech hedge that fringed the pavement, there were flashes of black beams and white stucco, a large pseudo-Tudor pile. Hell, she thought. Does Mullen really live there?

* * *

Mullen had had enough for one day, even though it was only mid-afternoon. Quite why Derek Stanley and Rose had had to stay so long to 'make sure you're all right,' he really didn't know. Or rather in Rose's case it was pretty blooming obvious. Stanley had clearly disapproved of the way she had fussed around him, insisting on making him some food. She had looked in his cupboards and reported herself more than satisfied by what she found. "I'll soon whip up something nourishing and nice." In fact most of the things she had used were jars and tins that the professor had left in his cupboards plus some salad stuff that Mullen had picked up from Abingdon a few days earlier. But it was, he had to admit, very edible. By the time she had delivered three plates onto the long kitchen table, Mullen, who had left hospital just as lunch was about to be served, had realised he was starving. So he had eaten eagerly and gratefully, while accepting that the questions and small talk which raged around him were part of the price he had to pay for their help. All he could do was wonder rather desperately how much longer it would be before they went.

In the end he had resorted to subterfuge. "I think I need to go upstairs and lie down," he said, hoping this would speed their departure. Rose had opened her mouth to say something, but it was Stanley who answered and, metaphorically speaking, dragged her out of the house to his car. Mullen didn't warm to Stanley, but in this case he was grateful.

* * *

Now that he had the house to himself again, Mullen should have felt relaxed. He tried walking around, taking in the panelled corridors and surprisingly cool bedrooms, full of sunlight and shadow and heavy furniture and classical busts. But all the silence did was accentuate how edgy he was feeling. In addition, his head was beginning to throb again. The hospital had given him some analgesics, so he took a couple with a glass of water, then a third for good luck. Even with the rising temperature outside, the house seemed insulated from the summer. Mullen shivered. He would go for a walk. The air would surely do him good and he would enjoy tramping through the woods. He had never lived anywhere near a wood before, but here on Boars Hill they were everywhere. He took a baseball cap off the coat stand in the hall and let himself out of the front door. He was blinded for several seconds and lowered his head, focusing on the gravel beneath his feet, as he walked towards the road, waiting for his eyes to adjust.

When he did lift his head, he saw a woman standing in the gateway, some ten metres away. There was a red car beyond her, blocking the exit. He didn't recognise her at first, not until she lifted her hands to her head and, with a theatrical flourish, removed her wig. Becca Baines, with her cascade of bright red hair, the woman he had seen most clearly through a camera lens, glared at him in silence.

He stopped, uncertain what to do. If he had ever attended a university course for private investigators — there was bound to be some such institution somewhere in America — then perhaps he would have been taught how to react when confronted by a furious woman who knows you've been spying on her with your photo lens. As it was, he had only his own experience and gut instinct to guide him. Imagine she's a difficult customer at the Meeting Place, he told himself. Except that people there might, on a bad day, be hostile to people in general, whereas this woman had a very personal reason to want to assault him with whatever piece of weaponry she had to hand. Not that she appeared to be armed. No knife, no gun, no jack handle from the boot of her car. Only a long black wig Cher would have been proud of.

"Becca Baines," he said, trying to establish verbal contact. If he could get her talking, his thinking went, then there was less chance of her doing something she — and indeed he — might regret.

She clapped her hands together in mock applause.

"I've already been clubbed once," he said. "Look!" He pointed to his head, as if the white bandage around it wasn't obvious enough. Then the penny dropped. "You? It was you?"

"I wish it had been." Her face was impassive. Neither a definitive 'yes' or 'no.' Then she began to walk towards him.

Mullen tensed. His head was pounding like a bass drum and he was feeling ridiculously hot. He lifted his hand to his forehead, which was clammy with sweat. "Look—" he began.

"Bastard!" she said, just before he fainted.

* * *

When the man you're about to tear limb from metaphorical limb collapses onto the gravel in front of you for no good reason, it inevitably changes things. Becca

Baines froze. But it was momentary, the result of disbelief. She was a woman who acted first — and sometimes regretted it later. She didn't freeze solid. That had never been her way, not even as a three-year-old when she had snatched her teddy from the wheels of an oncoming lorry loaded with straw bales.

She dropped to her knees and checked for a pulse. It was there, if a little slow. "Hey!" she snapped. "You're not allowed to die on me."

His eyes flickered open and shut, but otherwise he lay still, blank and uncomprehending, lost in some other world.

"Let's get you inside," she said. "You really can't lie here all day. Or I might be tempted to park my car on top of you."

Mullen's eyes flicked open again, but otherwise he continued to look like an idiot on morphine. Her joke was lost on him.

* * *

When Mullen woke he was lying on the top of his bed and the room was full of shadow. The curtains had been half drawn. A glance at his watch told him it was just past six o'clock. He stared at the ceiling, thinking of nothing until he became aware of a snoring sound in the room. He propped himself up on one elbow and saw Becca Baines asleep in the large upright chair. On his first day in the house he had dragged it into the room from its original positon on the landing because he liked it so much. It reminded him of an ancient wooden throne. He swung his legs over the side of the bed and stood up. He padded across towards the door. He needed the loo. Becca shuddered violently and woke up.

"Sleep well?" they each asked the other in unison, as if they had been practising for a play. She laughed. He nodded, conscious that his head was no longer throbbing.

After their respective dozes, they both realised they were hungry, so they agreed to walk down the road as far as the Fox and eat there. Like him, she opted for a rare steak and insisted they both drink only water. "Don't want you collapsing on me again."

Mullen thought collapsing on her wouldn't be at all unpleasant, but he didn't dare say so.

Then, like a long-married couple, they ambled side by side back to the house in the weakening light, companionable and not needing to touch. She got into her car. "You can stay if you like," he said, this time daring to say what he was thinking.

She shook her head and started the engine. "I have an early shift tomorrow." She reversed the car in a tight circle and put her head out of the window. "Another time." She ran her hand through her mane of red hair. "Maybe!"

Mullen stepped across in front of the car, blocking her path.

"What?" There was impatience in her voice. A woman of quick emotions.

"Tell me why you came."

Her face was suddenly serious. "To tell you to stop screwing up people's fun."

"Is that how you saw it?"

"Of course. It was definitely fun while it lasted."

In the last few hours Mullen had discovered for himself why Paul had so liked her, but why on earth had she liked him? He felt a sudden stab of jealousy. He leant forward, hand on the car roof, his face close to hers. "What about Janice?" He really wanted to know what made Becca Baines tick. "Did you not think about her?"

Becca revved the engine ridiculously loud. Mullen moved back.

She pushed her head further out of the window. "I also wanted to warn you that I wouldn't trust that Janice further than you can throw her."

He opened his mouth to ask why, but the Punto lurched forward like a dog let off its lead in a large open field. Wheels span. Gravel flew. A cat that had been snooping around the shrubbery scarpered. And then Becca Baines was gone.

Mullen stood watching long after she had disappeared from view. What did she mean? Was that jealousy talking? Or had Paul Atkinson told her stuff about Janice which changed things? He looked up into the sky and felt the first few spots of rain on his face.

* * *

By the time the woman had crossed Magdalen Bridge and reached the roundabout, she was soaked to the skin. There had been a few droplets of rain in the air when she had left the cocktail bar in the High Street, but this was a downpour. There was a pub across the road, but she had no desire to take refuge in there. Instead she walked across the side road which leads to St Hilda's College and then continued straight on, stomping along the Iffley Road, head down, hands stuffed deep into her coat pockets. She didn't care that she was soaked. Clothes will dry given a bit of time and a bit of hanging space. She wished all her problems were as easy to resolve as that.

Maybe two hundred metres further on she stopped and raised her head. She looked across the road and took in a block of modern-looking, architecturally unexciting flats. Beyond them there stood a short terrace of tall town houses, all arched windows and grey-brown brickwork; they were striking, but would 'benefit from some improvement' as an estate agency would have said. It was this set of four properties which held the woman's attention. She looked left. A car was parked some fifty metres away, side lights on, waiting for someone presumably, but it showed no sign of movement. Turning right, she saw three cars approaching. She studied them as they swished past. Even in the rain, their windows were open. Young women dressed in wild pink outfits thrust their heads through the windows and shouted coarsely at her. For a moment she wished she was one of them, off out on a hen night, to flirt outrageously with any men they encountered and to drink and dance until the last club was closed. But that wouldn't, of course, have solved anything.

She hunched herself even tighter against the rain and began to cross the road, reciting to herself for the umpteenth time what she was going to say when he opened the door. There were things she needed to tell him. There was stuff she needed to get off her chest. But she never did.

Chapter 5

Wednesday morning dawned bright and full of promise, the overnight rain only a memory. Not that Mullen knew anything about the dawn or heard the birds chorusing in the many trees which surrounded his Boars Hill home. He slept through it all, his dreams buried so deep they never rose anywhere near his consciousness. When he woke, the sun which shafted between the partially drawn curtains told him it was long past breakfast time. Nevertheless he pulled the duvet over his head and tried to ignore the morning light. Eventually it was his bladder which forced him out of bed. After that, he had no option but to face the day. He prolonged it by opting for a long bath — it seemed easier than trying to shower with his head bandage. After that, he took a bowl of muesli and a mug of tea into the garden at the back of the house.

Sitting there, hiding from the world, he found it impossible to ignore the fact that the grass seemed to be growing even as he looked at it. Keeping the lawns in order was one of the several tasks he had promised to do in lieu of rent. So Mullen, who liked to keep his promises, went to the shed and got out the mower. There was something immensely therapeutic in taming the garden.

After the lawns, Mullen found a strimmer and attacked the weeds which were threatening to encroach onto the gravel drive from under the rhododendrons and camellias. Then he turned his attention to the kitchen garden; someone had planted potatoes, runner beans, lettuces and beetroot. Mullen would never eat them all himself, but as he wielded a hoe around them, tiptoeing between the plants like a ballerina, he felt almost content. If only life could always be this simple.

Eventually he went inside and made himself a sandwich — cheese, ham and mustard. He had just taken a bite, sitting at the long kitchen table, when there was a heavy banging at the front door. He got up reluctantly. Whoever it was, he knew they were about to spoil his day.

"Hello, again." It was DI Dorkin, probably the last person in the world he wanted to see. And Dorkin was not in a good mood. "You like messing people around, Mullen?"

Mullen said nothing. It seemed more diplomatic in the circumstances.

The first finger of Dorkin's right hand prodded him on the sternum. "You said you lived in the Iffley Road!"

Mullen wasn't going to cave in to bullying. "I moved."

"You trying to play silly buggers with me, Mullen?"

Mullen reverted to silence. He thought it might be safer. Behind Dorkin stood a man Mullen hadn't seen before, presumably a detective constable or sergeant. But whatever his rank, structurally he was extremely impressive, six feet four if he was an inch and with the physique (and face) of an old fashioned bare-knuckle boxer.

"We'd like you to come to the station, if that is not too much trouble," the man-mountain said, deadpan.

Mullen nodded.

As for Dorkin, his mood suddenly appeared lighter, almost skittish. He smiled. "Or even if it is."

* * *

Doreen Rankin was used to her boss's erratic time-keeping. Arriving just in time for meetings was something he had developed into an art. "I'd rather sit at home in my pyjamas, do an hour or two on my laptop and then drive in after the rush hour." He had told her as much on the second day of her employment at GenMedSoft, just after he had appeared in his office at ten twenty-five in the morning. She had been in a mild panic because a man and a woman were sitting in reception, having arrived early for a meeting scheduled for ten thirty. "If you minimise wasted time, you maximise productivity," he concluded serenely. "And sitting in the traffic is wasted time."

So when he had still not turned up at ten forty-five that Wednesday morning, she was not unduly worried. Besides, she had had plenty to do, and it was only when the marketing director Eddie Loach rang up for the third time and complained that Paul wasn't answering his emails or his mobile calls that she decided she would have to intervene. In point of fact, Paul had two mobiles, but his personal one he kept personal. Only Doreen knew the number and even she used it very sparingly. She didn't like Loach and she certainly didn't trust him. He was a man who would cause trouble for Paul if he possibly could, and trouble for Paul would mean trouble for her. So she sent a text to Paul's personal mobile. There was no response. She waited ten minutes, during which time an external client in a bad mood rang to speak to Paul.

As far as she was concerned, that was enough. She dialled his mobile. After five rings, it cut into an answerphone message. Doreen killed the call and pursed her lips in irritation. She got up and shut her door firmly. If she had to leave an assertive message for him, she didn't want anyone wandering up or down the corridor to overhear. She rang again. She knew exactly what she would say to him. It was one thing for him to be 'maximising productivity' at home, but it was quite another not to keep her informed. It was something they had discussed at length before, but clearly he needed reminding. And when he rang her back, she wanted an apology from him too. She pressed the redial button and prepared to wait for the five rings.

"Hello?"

The immediate response caught her by surprise. But she recovered quickly. "Even by your standards, Paul, this is late."

There was an indistinct noise from his end of the line.

Doreen pressed on. "I can't protect your back if I can't get hold of you. Eddie is on the warpath and—"

"Stuff Eddie."

She opened her mouth to protest, but he ploughed on. "Haven't you heard the news?"

"What news?"

"Janice is dead."

"Dead?" Her mouth parroted the word, while her brain was trying — and failing — to comprehend what she had just heard.

"She was killed in the Iffley Road last night. A hit and run."

"Oh!" Doreen was still failing to come up with anything meaningful to say.

Paul Atkinson pushed on. "So you can tell Eddie the beagle that I won't be in today and I won't be answering his pathetic emails either." With that, he terminated the call.

* * *

"How's the head? Still hurting?"

Mullen nodded.

"Poor you!" Dorkin gave no impression that he meant it.

He and his tame gorilla — otherwise known as Detective Sergeant Fargo — were sitting opposite him in a characterless box of an interview room with puke-coloured walls. Fargo had already turned on the recording machine and completed the formalities. Now he was leaning forward, elbows on the table, as if ready to indulge in the chummiest of chats.

Dorkin was leaning back as far as he could go in his chair and seemed to be finding the whole thing highly amusing.

"What exactly do you want?" Mullen said trying to move things along. The two detectives had totally ignored him during the car journey from Boars Hill to the station, talking only to each other and even then only in one- or two-word sentences.

"Where were you last night?" Dorkin said. "Between eight p.m. and midnight."

"At home."

"For the benefit of the recorder, can you confirm that by 'home' you mean The Cedars, Foxcombe Road, a house owned by Professor and Mrs Thompson and in which you are currently living, in accordance with some privately agreed house-sitting arrangement." Dorkin spoke without urgency, a man who had the situation under control.

"That is correct."

"Are there any witnesses to where you were last night?"

It was then that Mullen knew something was wrong. Sitting in the car as they drove to Cowley, he had assumed that Dorkin merely wanted another go at him, to go over old ground again and maybe tell him to get his nose out of police business. But he wouldn't be asking questions about the previous night if that was the case. Mullen felt anxiety tighten around his chest.

"A friend and I went to the Fox for supper. She went home about nine thirty. I went to bed shortly afterwards."

"Does your friend have a name?"

"Yes."

"Are you going to tell us what it is?"

"No."

Dorkin twitched. It was a mannerism Mullen had noticed that evening at the Meeting Place. He wasn't sure what it meant, but it felt like a minor victory.

"Why not?" Fargo interrupted. He leant even further forward. Mullen could see that he took the role of bad cop pretty seriously. He smelt of sweat and pungent aftershave.

"Professional confidentiality," Mullen said, staring back.

"So he was a client?" Fargo said, seeing a gap and charging straight for it. "What were you doing for him?"

"No comment."

"Or was it a female client? Hiring you to spy on a husband?"

Mullen turned towards Dorkin. "Why don't you tell me what this is all about? Otherwise I might change my mind and ask for a solicitor."

Dorkin studied him for several seconds. Then nodded to Fargo. Fargo leant back, opened up a folder he had been cradling on his lap and produced two photographs which he slipped across the table to Mullen. Mullen felt the bile rising up his throat.

A few days ago it had been him pushing an envelope of photographs across the table to Janice Atkinson. Now he was on the receiving end and the person in the photos was Janice. Only Janice wasn't indulging in extra-marital high jinks with some admirer. Janice was beyond that. She was dead.

"Jesus!" Mullen said without thinking. "It's Janice. What the hell happened to her?"

"Hit and run."

"Do you know . . . ?" Mullen never finished his question. Obviously they didn't know who had done it or they wouldn't have hauled him in. Dorkin and Fargo were both watching him as if they didn't believe him. As if they thought he already knew about Janice's death. As if they thought he was involved in it. Anger rose in him like a rip tide. His hands gripped the table as if by so doing they could keep his impulses under control. His impulses were urging him to punch the hell out of Dorkin's smug face, but of course he wasn't stupid enough to do that, not here and not with Fargo eyeing him from across the table. Mullen looked down at the photographs again, forcing himself to study them, waiting for his emotions to recede. Poor Janice. Poor unhappy Janice.

"It happened on the Iffley Road," Dorkin said, all matter of fact. "Very near where you used to live, Mullen. Where we thought you lived until we discovered otherwise." He paused for several seconds. "I expect that was where Janice thought you lived too. Bit of a coincidence, don't you think?"

Mullen wasn't going to tell Dorkin what he thought.

"So, Mullen." Dorkin began to drum the table with his fingers. Was this him getting down to business? "Did Janice not know you had gone up in the world? Were you keeping it a secret from her? Didn't you want her following you up to Boars Hill?"

Mullen said nothing. If he started, he might never stop.

"You see, Mullen, the way I see it is this: either she's a client and you've been doing a job for her or you were lovers and you dumped her. Only she didn't like being dumped, did she?" Dorkin paused for as long as it took for his fingers to reach their crescendo. Then he pushed on. "So Janice came round to have it out with you. The only problem was that you weren't there. Unless, of course, you were; sitting in your car, with nasty thoughts running amok in your head. Perhaps you had even invited her round. And when you saw her struggling across the road in the pouring rain, you saw your chance and decided to take it."

"So take a look at my car!" Mullen was half-way up on his feet when he realised what he was doing. He was losing it, playing into Dorkin's hands. He forced himself back down into his seat. "See if you can find any damage to the bodywork." he said. "You won't."

"The pathologist says she was unlucky. It was only a glancing blow. So there probably wasn't much in the way of damage to the vehicle." Dorkin's almost permanent smirk had finally been replaced by a steely glare. "This is how I see it. She must have realised what was happening at the last minute. She nearly got out of the way. Only she didn't. The vehicle clipped her and when she fell her head cracked against the curb of the pavement. Good night, Vienna."

Mullen was confused. His thoughts were scrambled egg. Maybe he was entering some sort of shock. He had seen Janice in church only on Sunday, full of life and bitterness, desperate for his help. How could she be dead?

"So tell me how you know Janice." Dorkin had changed gear, his voice calm and reasonable.

Mullen didn't reply immediately. He didn't want to say anything and yet he knew he had to. Otherwise Dorkin would interpret it as refusing to co-operate and he would become the prime suspect. So keep it simple and straightforward, he told himself, or you'll end up tripping yourself up. "She hired me to find out if her husband was having an affair."

"And was he?"

"Yes."

"Who with?"

Again Mullen hesitated. But again he knew he had no choice. "A woman called Becca Baines."

"You have her address?"

"No," he lied.

"You didn't follow her home ever?"

"No. They always met at a hotel, that new one off the northern ring road. Why don't you ask Paul Atkinson? He must know."

"And I know how to do my job, thank you Mullen." Dorkin wasn't exactly cuddly in his manner, but now that he was in control and Mullen was co-operating, he was almost human.

"If this interview is going to continue any longer, I want a lawyer," Mullen said. It was a bit late in the day to say it, but he realised he had been stupid not to insist on it sooner. He was in danger of getting out of his depth.

"No need," Dorkin said. "You're free to go. We've finished talking — for now."

* * *

Mullen may have been free to go, but that still meant he was in Cowley, the best part of four miles from home — and from his car. It was on his car that his thoughts focused initially as he began the long walk which led into the city. No doubt Dorkin and Fargo had taken a good look at it before they hammered on his door, checking it for any signs of hit-and-run damage. They wouldn't have found any, of course. But even so, they had pulled him in. He didn't entirely blame them. Dorkin's assumption that Janice had come to the Iffley Road because she had wanted to speak to him seemed spot on. When Mullen thought about it that was the only conclusion he could come to himself, because he had never told Janice he had moved or was intending to. Rose knew, of course, and so did Derek Stanley, but unless one of them had told Janice, she almost certainly wouldn't have done.

Poor Janice. He wished he had been nicer to her. He wished he hadn't left her drinking on her own in the pub that day. He hadn't even bought her a drink! It wasn't as if he had to sleep with her, just be some sort of friend. Sit and listen for as long as it took. Still at least they had had a conversation in church. That was something. She hadn't seemed to hold any grudge.

Mullen paused, waiting as a supermarket home delivery van tried to exit Howard Street onto the Cowley Road. As he stood there another thought bubbled to the surface: if Janice didn't know he had moved, how come the police had found out so quickly? Someone must have told them. He hadn't told them he was moving either. He had given them his Iffley Road address the day he had found Chris in the river and he hadn't told Dorkin any different when he came to the Meeting Place. The police might have gone round to his Iffley Road address and found him gone, but he hadn't left a forwarding address there because he didn't see the point. He had no idea how long his arrangement with the professor would last. It was meant to be for nine months, but he found it hard to visualise that actually happening. When had he last lived in one place for that long?

Mullen pushed on. The Oxford Road had become the Cowley Road. He had just passed the Christian Life Centre and was approaching the beginning of the shops and restaurants that make Cowley Road the melting pot that it is. He was starving. His sandwich was lying on the kitchen table in Boars Hill — he had only managed one bite. He was also dying for a coffee. It didn't take long to find a place that suited his mood and had Wi-Fi. He decided on a ham and cheese panini and a skinny cappuccino and he sat at the back, out of the way. At first he concentrated on eating, but after that he wiped his hands carefully and got out his mobile. He went to the Oxford Mail website. It didn't take long to find what he wanted, a report on the hit and run. Janice had not been named — it was too soon for that — but the reporter had jammed plenty of information into a ten-line article. The incident had happened round about ten p.m. The driver had not stopped. It had been raining hard at the time. The police were appealing for witnesses.

But what was not in the article was of most interest to Mullen. It did not say that the police were looking for any particular model or colour of car. In fact, Mullen realised suddenly, the article used the word 'vehicle' not 'car,' which suggested that they had no idea what they were looking for and so, presumably, they had no witness of the moment of impact. Was it really likely that no-one had seen it? Maybe so, given the weather conditions. But

Mullen nevertheless felt uneasy. Was it paranoid of him to be suspicious? Chris dies in a river, his bloodstream full of alcohol when he had supposedly given it up. Janice is killed in a hit-and-run. Janice knew Chris, as did her husband Paul, not to mention Rose Wilby and Derek Stanley and plenty of other people from St Mark's. And why had Janice tried to find him at ten p.m. on a dreadfully wet evening when half the world was tuned into the World Cup and the other half were desperately flicking channels to find a programme that didn't involve an inflated pig's bladder. She must have had a pressing reason to do so, something she needed to tell him. Mullen didn't believe in coincidences. It would have to be one heck of a coincidence for Janice to just happen to be accidentally killed outside the building where he had been living. That didn't make him a conspiracy theorist as far as he knew. And he was pretty sure he wasn't paranoid, though now he came to think about it most paranoid people were probably unaware of it. All he knew was that something stank to high heaven.

* * *

Mullen took his time over a second cappuccino — followed by a second trip to the loo — before he finally headed off to look for witnesses. It wasn't that he was reluctant to do so, more a question of timing. He wanted to give himself the best opportunity of finding people in, which meant, he reckoned, not starting until six p.m.

He began with the terrace of old town houses in which he himself had temporarily stayed. They were all split into tiny bedsits and although a surprising number of people were in, he drew a total blank. Even Pavel, with whom Mullen had gone out for a drink a few times when he was living there, could only shrug his shoulders in sympathy. What with the foul weather, the prevalence of double glazing and the manifold attractions of the TV on such a night, no-one had apparently noticed when death had come careering down the Iffley Road the previous evening. One elderly couple thought they had heard a bang, but when the man had looked out of the window, he hadn't seen anything. One or two people had noticed the arrival of the police car and ambulance a few minutes afterwards, but that was all.

By seven thirty, Mullen was resigned to failure as he reached the top floor of a block of tired-looking flats named after a writer Mullen had never heard of. There were two doors there, as there had been on each floor below. After this, Mullen resolved, he would give up and go home. He rang the bell of the one on the right, but no-one answered even though there was light visible underneath the door and sound coming from a TV turned up very loud. He tried the door opposite. This opened immediately.

Mullen found himself looking at a curious-faced old woman, and he embarked on his spiel, explaining who he was and why he was there. He was expecting her at any moment to make her excuses and shut the door in his face, because that was the sort of evening he had been having. But on the contrary she beckoned silently, inviting him in as if this was something she did every night. She was notably thin, with a sharply pointed nose, a gentle voice and clothes that suggested a love of Scotland. "Do take a seat."

Mullen sat down in an armchair, while she manoeuvred herself into the one opposite him. Like her, the upholstery looked as though it could do with a few repairs.

"So," she said brightly. "You're looking for witnesses?"

Mullen nodded. "So far, no-one has seen anything." He didn't think it was going to be any different this time. The fact that she had asked him in signified nothing. He guessed she didn't get many visitors. She was lonely and she had dragged him in for some company and a chat. Not that Mullen minded. He was almost relieved.

"Well," she said, "of course I didn't see anything."

Mullen tried not to let his disappointment show. "Not to worry. Maybe—"

The old woman exploded into laughter, rocking back and forth with glee. "Haven't you noticed?"

Mullen looked at her, nonplussed. What was so funny? And then the penny dropped. "You're blind!" It was suddenly glaringly obvious.

"And you claim to be a private eye!" She laughed again, delighted with the situation, but abruptly switched it off. When she spoke again, it was with the utmost seriousness. "I heard the collision, you know."

"You heard it?" Mullen parroted, unconvinced.

"I may be blind, but I'm not deaf." She spoke without any sign of the irritation that she might reasonably have felt at Mullen's response. "Quite the contrary, I have very good hearing."

"Of course." Mullen felt chastised.

"I imagine it's a nice smooth ride. A quiet engine, but not so quiet I couldn't hear it."

Mullen frowned and then immediately wondered if she could hear a frown — or at least sense it. He hoped not.

Sitting there, in this slightly shabby flat, Mullen saw the old woman in a new light. He was pretty sure he must have seen her before. Maybe they had passed in the street and he had walked past her without even noticing. They had lived within 50 metres of each other, yet they might as well have been living in parallel universes. Mullen felt a sense of shame, but he also, for the first time that day, felt the beginnings of something like optimism. He leant forward, as if leaning forward might help him to grasp the importance of whatever it was she might say.

"You said you heard the collision," he said. "Can I ask you just to talk me through exactly what you heard? Was the car going fast? Did it brake sharply? Did the driver stop and get out of his or her vehicle? All the details."

She leant back in her chair, and drew in a deep breath, as if trying to recollect. "It was just after ten o'clock.

Maybe five past. I know because I had just finished listening to the radio. I turned it off, and opened the window. The rain was falling, but the wind had dropped. I like to listen to the city. I remember hearing some of the city bells striking the hour. Christchurch is always the last to finish. And I remember thinking how quiet it was. Not silent, you understand, it is never silent, but for Oxford it was very quiet. Then I became aware of someone in a hurry. She must have been a woman, because her heels were beating a tattoo on the pavement. As she got closer, she suddenly stopped, and then after a pause I heard her heels again, only the sound was slightly different. I think she must have been crossing the road, from the far side to the near side. Then I heard the car. I hadn't noticed it before, but the engine growled sharply as if the driver had rammed his foot on the accelerator. Then there was a thud. That must have been the poor woman being hit, though I wasn't sure at the time exactly what was happening. The car slowed down, but only briefly, and then it drove off away from town as if nothing had happened."

Mullen felt a spike of excitement. "I want you to think very carefully. Are you saying that the car didn't brake before it hit the woman?"

She replied without delay. "Oh no, I'm quite sure of that."

They both fell silent. Mullen shivered and looked across to the window. It was partially open. He tried to listen to the noise outside, as she must listen to it from her small secluded world — vehicles accelerating and braking, someone hooting in the distance, young women giggling, shoes clicking on the pavements, a male voice arguing violently with itself.

"So has that been any help?" the old woman asked eagerly.

"Help?" Mullen said. He had been miles away, as the hamsters powering the treadmill inside his brain struggled to get up to speed. "I should say so. Do you realise what you have just described?" But that was a rhetorical question and Mullen pressed on with his own answer. "You've described a car suddenly accelerating as the woman started to cross the road. A car that doesn't brake until after it has hit the person. What you've described isn't an accident. It's murder."

"Gosh! I suppose it is."

But it wasn't only Lorna Gordon — for that was her name — who was bubbling with excitement. Mullen stood up, unable to contain himself in the armchair. He strode over to the windows and looked down to where Janice Atkinson had died. He closed his eyes and tried to imagine it as it must have been for Lorna listening to it all happen: high heels clacking, an engine roaring into life, a dull thud as the car hit Janice's vulnerable bodywork. Mullen felt giddy and grabbed at the window frame, steadying himself.

"Would you like a cup of tea?" Lorna Gordon asked.

And Mullen, much to his own surprise, said he would.

* * *

Mullen delayed his departure from Lorna Gordon's flat for as long as he reasonably could, stringing out the mug of tea and accepting two chocolate digestives to go with it. While she chatted away, first about the hit-and-run and then about her grandson, Mullen's thoughts drifted. They centred initially on the prosaic task of getting home: he would have to walk into the city centre to get a bus out to Boars Hill. He wondered how frequent they were. But soon his ruminations moved on to Chris. Mullen realised with a start how little he had achieved in his investigation, though the word investigation seemed rather overblown for what he was doing. What exactly had he found out? Very little, except to establish that someone had been so annoyed by his attempts to track down where Chris had been living that they had slugged him over the head with something blunt and heavy. Mullen felt his bandaged head and resolved to take the thing off when he got home.

"Would you like another one?" Lorna Gordon leant down to pick up his empty mug.

"I really must be going."

"That's a shame."

Mullen stood up, but she hadn't finished yet.

"Are you going to tell the police?"

Mullen hesitated. He didn't like lying, especially to a woman as nice as Lorna. It went against all his instincts. And yet there were other moral imperatives by which he lived, such as protecting the weak. The last thing he wanted to do was to cause the police to come round and question her. The whole scenario made him feel uneasy.

"Well?" The old woman wanted an answer.

"Yes, of course I am. Don't you worry, I will tell them everything."

Mullen shook her hand and left, promising to come back and tell her all about it when they had caught Janice's killer. And when he said that, he really did mean it. One lie was enough.

* * *

Outside on the pavement, it was pleasantly warm. A gaggle of students in shorts and t-shirts walked past, heading out of town, talking animatedly. Mullen didn't take in what it was that had so caught their imagination because his eyes and attention were fixed on two figures who had, like him, just exited a building some 50 metres away, nearer town. The light was beginning to fade, but Mullen's eyes were keen enough to recognise the profiles — one tall, heavily muscled man in a suit and another shorter one, also in a suit, with untidy hair and an aquiline nose. Fargo and Dorkin. Mullen slipped into the shadows. On another day and in another place, he might have carried on walking right past them with a cheery greeting. But not tonight, not when they had just walked out of the building in which he had lived. What were they doing there? Checking his room? It seemed unlikely. Asking questions about him? It was much more likely that they had been checking him out. When exactly he had moved in and moved out, who he had socialised with, what visitors he had had.

The two detectives started walking towards town, little and large, still talking, to judge from the hand movements, though whether they were discussing work or the World Cup was anyone's guess. Across the road a couple walked arm in arm in the same direction, hurrying as fast as the woman's heels allowed. Mullen crossed over and settled in a few metres behind, using them as a protective screen. Not that he needed it. Fargo turned right at the next side street while Dorkin continued straight on without so much as a backward glance. He was walking faster now, a man on a mission to get home maybe.

Or maybe not, because when Dorkin got to the roundabout he turned right and pushed his way into the Cape of Good Hope pub. Mullen had had a pint there a couple of weeks previously, but it wasn't his sort of place. He'd be surprised if it was Dorkin's either, but maybe the detective was just thirsty. Mullen paused, uncertain what to do. What was Dorkin up to? Asking more questions? At this time of night in a busy pub? Or just delaying the moment when he returned home.

The couple who had been providing cover for Mullen had moved on, heading over Magdalen Bridge. A group of four Chinese — a man and three women — were standing in a huddle discussing something unintelligible. Mullen slipped behind them and felt in his pockets. He still had a packet of cigarettes left, so he lit one up in the pointless hope that it would somehow make him invisible. Across the road, through one of the large stone-framed windows, Dorkin suddenly came into view as he sat down with two pints. He pushed one across the table to a man Mullen didn't recognise.

The Chinese group had come to a decision and started to cross the road. Mullen followed them as closely as he dared. He wanted to get a better look at the man with Dorkin, maybe even go into the pub if he could without Dorkin spotting him. Yet if Dorkin did happen to catch sight of him, it wouldn't be the end of the world. After all, he could just be visiting a favourite haunt.

Mullen detached himself from the Chinese, who headed up the Cowley Road, and continued smoking his cigarette by the pub door. He'd give it a couple of minutes and then he'd go in and take his chance.

* * *

Mullen never did get inside the Cape of Good Hope because Dorkin's companion appeared in the doorway. He was breathing heavily. He turned round, as if worried that he was being pursued, swore and then shot across the road oblivious of any traffic exiting the Iffley Road. A taxi hooted. The man hurried on, arms flailing, across Cowley Place and onto the southern pavement of Magdalen Bridge. He was heading into the city centre. Mullen tossed his butt onto the ground and followed, but he crossed the Cowley Road taking the anti-clockwise route round onto the northern pavement of Magdalen Bridge, well out of view of Dorkin — or so he hoped.

Following the man couldn't have been easier. Along the curve of the High Street, turn right up through the pedestrianised Cornmarket, across Broad Street and into Magdalen Street. The man queued for a Kidlington bus and immediately struck up a conversation with a much younger woman he obviously knew from somewhere. Mullen slipped into the queue behind a pair of French-speaking youths. When the bus arrived, he bought a ticket for Kidlington. The man and woman — she was mid-twenties Mullen reckoned and, to judge from their conversation, his dental nurse — sat together. Mullen moved past them and slumped down in the seat behind.

He got out his mobile and pretended to check for emails. Not that he had any emails to check because he hadn't got round to linking his emails to his smart phone. He really should get a bit smarter with it, he told himself. What was the point of having it otherwise? At least he knew how to use the camera. He knew how to turn off the flash. He knew how to turn off the sound. In sum, he knew how to take a photo of two people talking animatedly to each other without either of them noticing.

The man got off just north of Summertown. The woman stayed seated, apparently bound for Kidlington. Mullen got off and followed the man at a distance down Victoria Road. The guy seemed too distracted and too lubricated with alcohol to have twigged him, but Mullen couldn't be sure. The man was halfway along the road when he slowed up. He had been swinging his arms like pistons, but now they dropped to his side and fell still. He pushed open a small gate, but went no further. The houses in Victoria Road are easy money for the local estate agents and the man was hesitating outside a particularly impressive one in Edwardian style. Money and status it said, which made Mullen all the more curious as to why a man like him should have been meeting Dorkin in a pub. He sure as heck wasn't a low-life informer. Mullen waited. The man, he realised, was being greeted by a woman, his wife presumably, though Mullen knew you should never make such assumptions nowadays. The man made as if to kiss her, but she appeared to duck away. She was talking and gesturing at the same time. An angry wife. An unhappy homecoming. These were reasonable deductions in the circumstances, Mullen told himself. Not that it mattered whether he was right or not because he had no intention of knocking on the door at this time of night. But he did want to know who the man was.

Mullen waited for the two of them to disappear inside and for the door to slam. He wandered along the pavement until he was in front of the house. There was a blue Audi A4 parked on the forecourt. He pulled out his phone and photographed the registration plate. As for the house number, that was easy enough to memorise. He hovered outside. The front curtains were drawn. What now? Maybe he would return next morning and follow him to work. Mullen was reviewing his options when a noise made him turn. A young man came out of the neighbouring house, slamming the door. He was thin and on edge. He immediately lit up a cigarette. That was one option. Ask him. Why not? Mullen got out his remaining packet and extricated a cigarette.

"Excuse me, mate," he said. "Can you spare a light?"

The youth looked at him as if he had been asked if he knew the quickest route to Timbuktu. Mullen held the cigarette up, a man miming the act of smoking. The youth shrugged and handed over his box of matches. Mullen lit his cigarette, choked violently like a schoolboy having a first smoke behind the bike sheds and handed the box back.

"You know who lives here?" He tried to make it casual and unimportant.

"He's my neighbour. Of course I do."

"I thought I recognised him. Not that Richard Dawkins fellow is he?"

The youth laughed as if that was the funniest thing he had heard all week. "Why should I tell you? And who the hell are you anyway?"

Mullen had been half expecting the response. In the youth's shoes, he would have said exactly the same. Mullen put his hand into his pocket and pulled out the cigarette packet again. And added a twenty pound note. There was no point in skimping.

He held them up, out of reach of the youth. "Who is he and what does he do? I can always ask someone else."

The youth was tempted, Mullen could see that. The money would buy him something a bit more exciting to smoke than tobacco if that was what he liked. Mullen was pretty sure he did like.

The youth held out his hand. "You first."

Mullen hesitated, and then handed over the cigarettes. The youth checked the packet and thrust them into his back pocket.

"First name: Alexander." The youth held out his hand again.

Mullen held out the £20 note.

The youth took a final pull on his cigarette before tossing the butt onto the pavement. Then he took the note and looked at it intently, as if suspicious that it might have been printed that morning in Mullen's backroom. Then he began to rip it up. One, two, three. He let the pieces flutter to the ground. "I don't sell out my neighbours, dickhead." He stared Mullen full in the face. It was a challenge, full of stupid bravado. Mullen knew he could flatten him with one blow, but what good would that do either of them? Actually, at some level he admired the cocky bugger for standing up to him.

The youth sneered, pleased with his performance and Mullen's feebleness. Then he retreated inside his front door. Mullen heard the lock click into place and the rattle of the security chain. Not so confident after all.

Mullen stayed where he was, sucking in a lungful of smoke. It was the second cigarette he had smoked that evening and the second since he had left the army nearly three years previously, but oddly enough it felt a bit of a let-down. He didn't miss the nicotine rush any more. Coffee was a different matter: he couldn't live without the buzz of caffeine at least three times a day. But fags had never held him in their thrall. Smoking had been something he had done while drinking a pint, nothing more. He tossed the butt towards the youth's door. It was petty, he knew, but if he got a telling off from his mum or dad in the morning, it would serve the cocky punk right.

Mullen wasn't done yet. He had had an idea. As ideas went, he couldn't see much wrong with it. He checked up and down the pavement: not a dicky bird. There was no sign of activity from either the youth's house or that of the man he had been stalking. The curtains were drawn in both front rooms. There were no twitching fingers to be seen and no curious faces peering out. Both houses had their recycling bins facing each other, as if by mutual agreement, down the side of their houses. Mullen padded quickly over to the one by his quarry's house and opened it. He peered into the shadows and then plunged his hand down. It was like the bran tub of childhood fetes. When he pulled his hand out, he had in his fingers a sheaf of papers. These included several envelopes and letters discarded without any attempt to tear or shred them. Which was careless, Mullen reckoned. But how many people bothered to shred their post, despite all the scare stories about ID theft? Mullen flicked through his haul and was reassured. He closed the bin's lid quietly and headed off up the road. He had lost twenty quid and his last packet of fags. He had had his chain pulled by a spotty sixth-former. But in other respects it had been a successful evening. All he had to do was catch two buses home.

* * *

The mystery man's name was Charles Speight. The envelopes recovered from the bin in Victoria Road were addressed variously to him, a Mrs Rachel Speight and a Jane Speight — a daughter presumably. Back in Boars Hill, Mullen made himself a mug of strong tea and opened up his laptop. It didn't take long searching the internet to identify Charles Speight in greater detail. He was a pathologist, privately educated at a school that even Mullen had heard of, and he had a string of letters after his name. There were several references to him in the Oxford Mail and Oxford Times, all of which indicated that he worked closely with the Thames Valley police in cases involving violent death. There were even a couple of photographs of him which, despite their formality, tied in with the rather agitated figure Mullen had first seen in the pub.

Mullen sipped his tea and wondered. Why had Speight and Dorkin met in a pub, out of hours and well away from their normal places of work? Was it Speight who had examined Chris? The newspapers hadn't said as much. Probably at this stage the police wouldn't release the information. But it seemed to Mullen a pretty good bet that he had. And if he had and if that was why he and Dorkin had met up, how come Speight had looked so on edge? Or had they been talking about Janice? Less than twenty-four hours after her death? Unless they were great buddies — and to Mullen it looked like they were anything but — why would they be meeting in a pub? And why had Speight stormed out of the pub so quickly and unhappily? The only way to find out would be to ask him, Mullen concluded, though that would surely get him into a whole shit heap of trouble if Speight went and bleated to Dorkin. Which he surely would, Mullen told himself, unless of course Speight had nothing to hide and nothing to feel guilty about.

Mullen pushed away his half-drunk mug of tea, conscious of a return of the pain at the back of his head, thumping like a bass drum. He had to speak to Speight. That was the bottom line. The only outstanding questions were how, when and where? He hoped the answers would become clear after a decent night's sleep.

Chapter 6

Mullen's mobile rang while he was asleep. He was back in the army, in Ben's bedroom. He had just opened the door. Ben was sitting at his small table with the red, blue and white angle-poise lamp his parents had brought him on their last visit. He had been so pleased with it. And then Ben had turned round. "Hello, mate," he said. Which was pretty odd because he didn't have a mouth to say anything with. There was just a huge black hole in his face. His nose had disappeared into it too. Only his eyes remained and they were closed. That was when the fire alarm had sounded right behind Mullen's head, except in reality it was his mobile phone.

For several seconds Mullen didn't move. Then he sat up and realised his pyjamas were drenched with sweat. He picked up the phone. It was a number he didn't recognise. It was 7.45 a.m. Who on earth rings people up at that hour of the day? He looked at the number for several seconds and then he powered the phone off. He took off his pyjamas, tossed them on the rug and got back into bed, pulling the duvet over his head.

He didn't get back to sleep. He lay there pretending to himself that he was asleep, because if he was he wouldn't have to do or think anything. Maybe at one point he almost did drift off into a half-doze. Or maybe not. Perhaps he would have stayed there all morning or even all day. It wouldn't have been the first time. But there was a heavy knocking on the door. That was what a brass knocker did — gave the visitor a chance to make a lot of noise. Mullen pulled on a pair of pants and his brown towelling dressing gown, before stumping down the stairs as the knocking reached a third crescendo.

"All right, hold your horses whoever you are!" Mullen shouted the welcome as he struggled to undo the bolts at the top and bottom of the door. Nothing seemed to be working right this morning. The chances were it was either the police again or — most likely, Mullen reckoned — Becca Baines, all primed to give him an ear-bashing because he had passed her name on to Dorkin and the police had hauled her into the station. But what alternative had he had?

Mullen wrenched the door open. He was wrong. The person banging the knocker as if his life depended on it was Derek Stanley. He was smartly dressed as usual — pale blue chinos, yellow and white striped shirt and linen jacket — but he seemed on edge. Behind and below him, one delicate foot on the bottom step, stood Margaret Wilby, dressed in a blend of light blues — blouse and slacks, cardigan and sandals.

"Hope we didn't wake you up, Mr Mullen?" she said.

"Can I help?"

"Why don't you go and make yourself decent," she said, advancing until she was millimetres from him.

Mullen retreated. He could see no option.

She sniffed. "Maybe even have a quick shower," she said. "We are not in a rush."

* * *

By the time Mullen had taken a super-quick shower, thrown some clothes on and got downstairs again, his two visitors had made themselves comfortable in the large kitchen with mugs of tea.

"One for you too," Margaret Wilby said, pointing to a mug on the table in front of an empty chair. Mullen sat down. The two of them were positioned opposite him, neat and stern, appraising him and finding him wanting. Shades of the Apprentice programme on TV. Mullen had watched it occasionally and been fascinated by the ridiculous nastiness of it all. In this case Margaret Wilby was the Lord Sugar figure while Derek Stanley was one of his minions, ready to add his two pennyworth when asked, but otherwise eminently forgettable.

"We were wondering how your investigations were going, Mr Mullen."

"Into Chris's death, you mean?"

"Of course."

Mullen picked up his mug and took a sip. He continued to hold it in both hands, a barrier against the woman's inquisition. "I only discuss the progress of the investigation with the person who hired me. In this case, your daughter."

"As you know, Mr Mullen, several people in the church contributed to your fee."

"Did you, Mrs Wilby? My impression was that you disapproved."

Margaret Wilby's lips pressed tight in irritation. Disapproval seemed to be part of her DNA.

"I contributed," said Derek Stanley, giving a reason for his presence.

Mullen stood up. "Even so, I'm still not discussing the case with you, not without Rose being present. Now, if you don't mind I'm going to make myself some toast. I've not eaten yet."

Mullen located two slices of wholemeal bread from the larder, put them in the toaster and removed marmalade and soya spread from the fridge. There was silence as he worked away, smearing his pieces of toast and then cutting them diagonally into triangles. Then he returned to the table and started eating as if they were no longer there. But if he hoped they would get the message and go, it didn't work.

"It's such a shame about Janice." Margaret Wilby spoke in the same tone of voice that she very likely used when discussing the weather. "Such a shame it rained today."

Mullen took another bite and refused to make eye contact.

"Actually," Stanley interrupted, "maybe in retrospect it's a good thing."

This time Mullen did look up. "What on earth do you mean by that?" He felt, he suddenly realised, very defensive about Janice Atkinson. She had come to him in need and he had at some level failed her. He had done what she had paid him to do, yet he had done nothing more. Guilt clung to him, which made it impossible for him to sit there quietly while a jerk like Derek Stanley spouted stuff like that.

"Janice and Chris." Stanley shrugged and allowed his face to do the talking. Enough said. Work it out for yourself, Mr Private Investigator.

"You're telling me Janice and Chris had an affair?"

"That is a blunt way of putting it, Mr Mullen." Margaret Wilby was taking back control. Or maybe she had been in control all along and Stanley was part of it — her tame stooge. "Chris was a very charming man. A bit of a rogue too, but what woman doesn't like a charming rogue? Poor Janice, with her marriage in tatters, was very susceptible to him. Of course, I don't know the precise nature of their relationship, but my impression is that she was making rather a fool of herself."

Mullen considered this as he finished the third quarter of his toast and took another slug of tea. "When you say her marriage was in tatters, are you saying you knew Paul Atkinson was having an affair?"

"Not at all. What I meant was that it was perfectly obvious from the way they behaved in public, from what they said and didn't say, that their relationship had entered rocky waters. And it was perfectly obvious too that Janice liked Chris. Dangerously so."

"So what exactly is your point?"

"I would have thought that was obvious."

Mullen was getting to like her less every time she opened her mouth. But hidden somewhere amid the unpleasantness was information about Chris that might be relevant — if it was true. "Humour me, Mrs Wilby."

She sniffed. "Personally, I don't go along with Rose's conspiracy theory about Chris. He had a relapse. He got extremely drunk, fell into the river and drowned. My daughter may not wish to believe it, but it happened. The pathology report supports that. His bloodstream was swimming with alcohol. The only issue as far as I can see is whether there was anyone else present at the time. My guess would be that if anyone was involved in it, if anyone did facilitate him in getting into such a state, it was Janice."

Guess was the operative word as far as Mullen was concerned. Possibly even an intelligent one. But nothing more than that. "Do you have any actual evidence, Mrs Wilby?"

"Do you, Mr Mullen?" She stood up and picked up her bag from the table. She had had her say and — to Mullen's relief — was going to leave. "I merely present to you what I know and what I consequently deduce. I suggest you give up your investigation with good grace and get back to more profitable work, such as tracking errant husbands. I do not want my daughter wasting any more money on a wild goose chase."

Mullen stood up too. He was not going to give her the satisfaction of having the last word. "Let's just get this straight, Mrs Wilby. You think Janice felt guilty about Chris? That she felt she had somehow driven him to drink and so to his accidental death?"

She didn't reply, though there was a slight nod of her head, as if in agreement.

"So how does Janice's own death fit in with that?"

She sighed, as if the whole conversation had become just too irritating for words.

"Suicide, Mr Mullen. She was so riddled with guilt that she walked into the path of an oncoming car. Maybe it was a split second decision. She saw the car coming her way in the rain and the dark and she just decided to end it all."

* * *

As Mullen watched the two of them disappear down the drive in Derek Stanley's blue Astra, his overriding emotion was one of relief. But there was another feeling too; it had at first been a mere grain of sand in his shoe, but as the minutes passed it had become a sizeable lump of sharp grit impossible to ignore. Earlier, lying in bed, he had been ready to give up. But Margaret Wilby, far from putting him off, had ironically achieved quite the opposite. For a start, he hadn't liked her hectoring, I-know-better-than-you manner. The more she tried to persuade him to give up, the more he felt determined not to. That was human nature, or his human nature at any rate. It was Rose who had hired him and he would stop only if Rose asked him to. And yet even if she did ask, even if she rang up this very moment and told him that they were quits, he wasn't sure he would. Because the death of Janice had changed things. Now it felt extremely personal.

Besides, Mullen mused, as he wandered round the back of the garden to review the tomato plants, he had been struck by something that Margaret Wilby had said. She had referred to 'the pathology report' on Chris. Those had been her precise words. It was almost as if she had had access to it or as if she had spoken to someone who did. She had, in their first meeting when she had given him lunch, hinted at being well connected; maybe she was. Did she know Charles Speight? Was he the pathologist who compiled the report on Chris? Was he working on Janice too? Why had Charles Speight been meeting Dorkin in a pub and why had that meeting been so brief? The questions flooded in, each demanding precedence in Mullen's reluctant brain. And out of those questions there took shape another one: what are you going to do about all of this, Mr Mullen?

The answer to that was in a sense rather modest. Mullen made a telephone call to the Reverend Diana Downey, though only after some considerable deliberation while he drank a fresh mug of tea at the kitchen table. His initial impulse had been not to ring her. Why give her advance warning that he was coming? Or indeed an opportunity to make an excuse not to see him? Better just to turn up at the vicarage or the church. Either she would be in or she wouldn't. Of course, said the pessimist inside Mullen, Thursday might be her day off. Did vicars have a standard day off? Unlike their congregation, it could hardly be a Sunday. Saturdays were often wedding days. So, he guessed, Thursday was as likely as any other, a one in five chance. Mullen imagined that vicars generally made a point of getting out of the parish on their day off, in order to avoid the unwelcome parishioner knocking on the door ('Sorry, Rev, but I wonder if I could just . . .'). Or did Diana Downey prefer to draw the curtains, microwave some popcorn and settle down on the sofa to catch up on the last series of Downton Abbey or Breaking Bad or whatever it was that floated her boat?

But in the end, after all the wondering and all the procrastination, Mullen made the call. She picked up on the third ring.

"Mr Mullen, how nice to hear from you."

Mullen was ridiculously pleased to hear these simple words. They made him feel like he was making Diana Downey's day. He had half expected her to have forgotten him altogether.

"I wonder if I could call round today?" he said.

"Today?" There was a pause, the sort of pause people who are caught on the hop make when they are trying to come up with a convincing excuse. Mullen cursed silently. It was a mistake to have rung her. Then, out of the silence, she spoke again. "How about half-two this afternoon?"

"Okay." He wondered if his surprise was obvious from his tone of voice.

"Is that all?"

"Yes. Thank you."

"My pleasure." Diana Downey hung up.

* * *

Becca Baines had known that the police would come looking for her. Once Mullen had told them about her fling with Paul, it could only be a matter of time. Of course the police tramping into the hospital in their clodhoppers — and didn't the huge DS Fargo have some big clodhoppers — meant that the news would be round the hospital faster than a bush fire in a bone-dry Australian summer, but that didn't ultimately matter.

At least Melanie Yarnell had had the sensitivity to give them some privacy from prying eyes by lending them her office, but Becca knew she would want something in return. From her point of view, the detectives' timing could hardly have been worse. She had been on shift for three hours — very busy and not a chance to grab even a cup of tea and biscuit — and she could feel her irritability level rising with every passing minute. On the other hand, she was getting an unexpected chance to sit down.

"Sorry to bother you," DI Dorkin began. Becca reckoned it was probably the least original gambit in his detective's book of easy interview openings. She was tempted to say so out loud, but Dorkin did not appear to be the sort of man who would appreciate such pleasantries.

"I don't suppose this will take long," he continued, in similar vein. "As long as you answer our questions satisfactorily."

It wasn't a line of conversation that filled Becca with any confidence. She imagined it was precisely the sort of thing the Gestapo must have said before they started torturing their prisoners.

"We understand that you and Paul Atkinson have a sexual relationship."

"Had," she said quickly.

"Had?" Dorkin frowned as if surprised or unconvinced. "So when did it start?"

If you are going to lie, keep it to an absolute minimum. Becca couldn't remember who had first advised her along those lines, but it had become, if not part of her DNA, then second nature.

"Five or six weeks ago, I guess."

"Guessing isn't good enough."

She pursed her lips as she weighed up her response. "We met at the hospital on the fifth of May. I was buying myself a coffee in the canteen. I had just paid for it when I dropped my cup. He kindly bought me another."

"Just like that?" Dorkin sounded very unconvinced.

"No, not just like that. I was giving you the shortened version so as not to waste valuable police time." Her irritability and facetiousness were breaking through. She knew it, but she didn't care. "The coffee went all over the floor and partially over my trousers. The left trouser leg to be precise. I freaked a bit. I think I swore. But he was right behind me in the queue and came to my rescue. He offered to buy me another coffee. I thought it was very kind of him."

"Did you now." Dorkin was still unconvinced. Becca could sense it, but she didn't mind. Maybe it was the two sugars in her tea, but she felt calmer now.

"Well, it wasn't pure altruism on his part. Obviously he fancied me. He wasn't the first man to stare at my chest and he won't be the last." She looked hard at Dorkin, then at Fargo and then back to Dorkin again, daring them to look at her breasts. To her surprise Fargo flushed in embarrassment. Dorkin merely sucked his teeth and resumed his questioning. "So when exactly did your relationship with Paul Atkinson finish?"

"After his wife found out, of course."

"Which was when?"

"Didn't Paul tell you? I presume you have already spoken to him."

Dorkin said nothing. He leant back in his chair and rubbed his hands together. Becca wasn't sure what that meant. But clearly they must have interviewed Paul and he would have spilt the beans about them. She guessed they wanted to compare stories and see what discrepancies they could unearth.

"He rang me on Monday. We didn't actually speak. He left a message on my mobile. All very short and not so sweet."

Dorkin perked up at this last comment. "So you didn't like it?"

She laughed. "I didn't like the fact that he hadn't got the balls to tell me face to face. I didn't like the fact that he left a voice message ending it. It was better than a text, I suppose, but only just. But actually — and I dare say you won't want to believe me — I was relieved. I knew it wasn't going anywhere. I was only ever going to be his bit on the side. I'm looking for more than that now."

"So why get involved with him in the first place?" Dorkin could sense the weakness of her argument. "He's an older married man, a recipe for disaster if you're looking for true love."

Becca knew he was right, but she wasn't going to admit it. "I wasn't looking," she said. "It just happened." She took two more sips of tea, buying herself a few seconds of thinking time. "Where were you on Tuesday evening, between eight and eleven o'clock?"

"That's easy. I was out. I had a meal with a friend. That was about eight. Then we walked back to his place and I drove home. I guess that was around half past nine or a bit later."

"Can anyone verify what time you got home?"

She shrugged. "Probably not. I live on my own in Wood Farm. Still I expect you've already found that out. You wouldn't be much good at your job if you hadn't."

Dorkin said nothing. He was watching her with half-closed eyes, waiting for her to slip up. "You've probably checked my car over too. In which case you'll not have found any evidence that I ran Janice Atkinson down. If you check the CCTV, you'll find I didn't drive along the Iffley Road that evening. And if you check your brains, you'll realise that I had no reason to even wish her dead."

Fargo stirred, scraping the floor with his chair as he did so. Unlike Dorkin, he had run out of patience. "Not if you're lying about your feelings. Not if you were so obsessed with Paul Atkinson that you'd do anything to free him from his wife."

Outside in the corridor there was an argument going on, loud enough to distract all three of them. As if by some tacit agreement, they waited for the bitter words to cease and for angry steps to mark the departure of both participants.

Then Dorkin resumed. "Who was this 'friend' you had supper with on Tuesday night? And where did you eat?"

"In the Fox pub on Boars Hill. It's not bad. Have you ever tried it?"

She watched with pleasure as the penny dropped with a clang inside Dorkin's head. She looked at Fargo. He didn't seem to have got it.

"And the friend I ate with was Doug Mullen. I think you know him, don't you? Anyway I am sure he will vouch for me."

* * *

An hour or so later, after some more work in the garden followed by a cheese sandwich, Mullen locked up the house and headed into Oxford. He parked in what was fast becoming his usual place in Lincoln Road, before walking briskly towards town, this time avoiding the main road — up Wytham Street, past the outdoor swimming pool and along Marlborough Road. Then he turned left, walking along the river until he reached the encampment. His hope was that the two men he had talked to just before he was clubbed into unconsciousness would be there. It was a long shot, he knew, and his fears were fulfilled. There was no sign of them at all. Only a guy with long lank hair who had clearly been smoking dope and was very likely going to be no use at all.

Even so, Mullen offered him a cigarette and lit it for him. "I'm Doug," he said, trying to get a conversation going.

"Fets," came the reply in thick Glaswegian.

"Fitz," Mullen replied, checking.

The man nodded and took a drag.

Mullen explained that he was trying to find two men: a tall skinny one with a scar down the side of his face and a shorter fatter man with tartan trousers and a Midland accent. The mention of the tartan trousers seemed to mean something to Fitz. He held out his right hand and stroked the palm with the index finger of his other hand. Money! Mullen swore to himself. He had had enough of handing out money and cigarettes to all and sundry and getting very little reward. But the man scratched at his palm all the more. "Gone." he insisted. "Liverpool."

Suddenly Mullen realised what he was saying. He wasn't asking for money. He was saying the two guys — or the tartan-trousered one at least — had come into some money and gone. It wasn't good news. Liverpool wasn't exactly local. Had they been paid to move on by whoever had knocked him unconscious and stripped Chris's tent of all its possessions? It seemed more than possible. Mullen pulled out his last packet of cigarettes. There were only seven left in it, but the guy had earned it. He handed it over. He also handed over one of his own business cards. It was the longest of long shots, but you never knew. "Ring me if either of them ever comes back and it'll be worth twenty quid. All right?"

The man nodded. Mullen turned away and then suddenly back again. It was stupid not to ask. "Did you know Chris?" Fitz stared at him uncomprehending. Mullen continued. "He drowned in the river down near Sandford. He had long fair hair, was tall and wore a camouflage jacket and trousers. He had a tent here." Mullen waved his arms around in the hope that this might somehow prompt the man. But he merely stared back at Mullen, face and eyes blank, and muttered 'Liverpool' again. If he had known Chris, it might as well have been in another universe.

* * *

Despite walking with deliberate slowness along the river, Mullen arrived at the vicarage a quarter of an hour before the agreed time. He hated being late, but even he recognised that this was ridiculously early. If he wanted to get off on the wrong foot with the Reverend Downey, then knocking on her door fifteen minutes before she was expecting him would almost certainly achieve it. He paused, wondering whether to do a circuit of the area or go and buy another bar of chocolate from the woman who had been so helpful in the shop down the Abingdon Road. Not for the first time in his life, chocolate won.

Or chocolate would have won if something very unexpected had not occurred. Mullen had just checked his wallet for money when the front door of the vicarage opened. His first instinct was to raise his hand and call out — after all he knew the man well enough to do so. But there was something about the way Kevin Branston emerged from the house — not exactly furtive, but not exactly unfurtive either — which caused Mullen to hold back. If Branston had turned west, then they would inevitably have seen each other. But he didn't. And as Mullen watched him hurry off in the direction of the Abingdon Road as fast as his weight would permit, it was with a bewildered sense of excitement that maybe he had been witness to something he really hadn't been intended to see. Had Branston been getting out of the vicarage in plenty of time to avoid bumping into him? Surely, Mullen debated with himself, he wasn't being paranoid to think that?

* * *

As Mullen gave up on the chocolate and retreated back along the river, he wrestled with his thoughts. Kevin Branston knew Diana Downey. He hadn't known that. But was that so much of a surprise? Both of their jobs included dealing with the marginalised of Oxford. Chris had attended both St Mark's and the Meeting Place. Was that just because they were places where he could get a welcome and free food? Or had Chris had connections with Branston and Downey that went back further? These were the thoughts that ricocheted wildly around his head right up to the moment when at 2.31 p.m. he finally knocked on the vicarage door.

Diana Downey welcomed him with a smile. Nothing surprising in that. It was part of her professional persona, and yet Mullen couldn't help feeling that she seemed a bit on edge.

"It's kind of you to see me at such short notice," he said, trying to lay his own distracted thoughts aside.

"Not at all. Would you like a cup of tea? Or coffee?"

"I'd like to talk about Chris." Mullen knew as soon as the words came out of his mouth that they wouldn't win a good manners competition, but he didn't much care.

"Okay."

They went into what was clearly her study — desk, laptop computer, multi-function printer, bookshelves, a wooden cross on the wall, a slightly bedraggled orchid on the window sill and at the far end of the long room a low round table with two armchairs either side. She waved him to one of them while she sat in the swivel chair by the desk.

"So what do you want to know?" She was sitting upright, facing him, hands clasped over her lap, looking directly into his face. Her chair gave her a distinct height advantage and her whole demeanour spelt out an underlying message: this is a business meeting — nothing more and nothing less.

Mullen plunged straight in. "Did you ever smell alcohol on Chris's breath?"

"No." There wasn't even a hint of hesitation.

"You never saw him drinking alcohol?"

"No."

"Not even at Communion?"

This time there was, Mullen reckoned, a fractional hesitation before Diana Downey replied. "He never took communion."

It was Mullen who paused now, but deliberately so. He wanted to be sure he phrased this next bit right. It was a crucial moment. "Was anyone in the church having an affair with Chris?"

Diana Downey opened her mouth as if to speak. But at that very moment, like some divine intervention, the phone on the desk rang. She turned and grabbed it as if it was a lifebelt.

A man spoke. That it was a man was clear enough to Mullen. The man tried to plunge straight into a conversation, but she cut across him. "I'm in a meeting. I'll ring you back when it's over. In half an hour or so." She replaced the phone and swung round to face Mullen. "The answer to your question, Mr Mullen, is that I very much doubt it. Of course, my parishioners do not keep me abreast of all their sins and failings, but usually I find out in the end. People like to confess."

"And I suppose if anyone had confessed to you, in your capacity as a priest, you wouldn't feel able to tell me anyway."

She inclined her head, but said nothing.

"My impression was that people liked Chris." Mullen was not going to let her off that easily. "Why else would people in your church have hired me to find out how he ended up dead in the river? He must have been an intriguing newcomer. Attractive to women I imagine. A bit of a mystery man. Even good Christian women must have been tempted."

The Reverend Downey licked her lips. Her eyes stared back at his. "No-one is exempt from temptation, Mr Mullen."

No-one? Mullen had a wild thought: had Diana fancied Chris herself? She must be about forty, so not much older than him. Unless of course she was more interested in women? After all there didn't appear to be a Mr Downey.

Diana Downey broke into his speculations. "Any other questions?"

Mullen lowered his head and clasped his hands to his temples. He groaned softly.

"Are you all right, Mr Mullen?"

He shook his head and opened his eyes. "Do you by any chance have any pain killers? My head."

"Of course. I'll go and find some."

"And maybe I can take you up on the offer of a cup of tea. Two sugars."

"Of course." Diana Downey was on her feet and out of the room. He heard her filling a kettle. Then she was heading upstairs, presumably to find some pills.

Mullen stood up and walked over to the desk. He picked up the phone, dialled 1-4-7-1 and waited. "Telephone number 01865 . . ." He memorised the six numbers that followed the Oxford STD code. He heard footsteps on the stairs. It was Diana Downey returning. He slipped the receiver back onto its stand and returned to his chair, just as she appeared in the doorway.

"Paracetamol or aspirin?"

"Either," he said weakly, as if he was beyond making even such a simple decision.

"I'll just get the sweet tea and some water as well."

* * *

Mullen felt bad. He wasn't someone who took pleasure in deception. And he wasn't sure he was very good at it. But it was a case of needs must. The man who had rung Diana had called himself Charles. Mullen was pretty sure about that. "Hi, it's Charles." Those had been his words. Then "I just wanted—" before she cut him short and promised to ring back.

Two days ago he had followed a Charles Speight home from a meeting with Dorkin. Today Diana Downey is rung by a Charles she doesn't want to speak to in front of Mullen. Was it the same Charles or a different one? A mere coincidence or something more significant?

"How are you feeling?" It was Diana Downey, returning after another disappearance upstairs. After doling out three paracetamol tablets — "an extra one won't hurt" — plus water, a cup of tea and two biscuits, she had retreated and spent a surprisingly long time in the loo. Now she was back.

"Definitely a bit better," he replied with what he hoped was a weak smile. "I didn't sleep so well last night. Then I decided the garden needed some attention this morning and I never got round to eating, so it's all my own stupid fault."

"Not your fault that someone slugged you over the head."

"You heard about that?"

She grinned. "There's nothing like a church grapevine."

Mullen sipped at his tea.

"So," she said. "I don't mean to sound unwelcoming, but I have a meeting in twenty minutes. Do you want me to organise a lift for you?"

"Thank you. I'm sure I'll be OK. I've got my car."

"No more questions?"

"One, if you don't mind." Or even if she did.

She waited, hands pressed together as if she was preparing to pray.

"Did Janice like Chris?"

Diana Downey hesitated before she gave a measured reply. "By 'like' I presume you mean was she sexually attracted to him?"

"Yes."

She pondered the question for several seconds, pushing an unruly lock of hair back with her right hand. Eventually she stood up, as if to signal that this really was the last question. "My understanding, Mr Mullen, was that it was you she was most attracted to."

Mullen was thrown off balance. He had thought he had control of their interview, but a single riposte had him floundering. Of course, Diana Downey was right that Janice had been attracted to him. But who had told her? Or was it an open secret round the church? Was that the reason why he had received so many curious looks on Sunday?

Mullen stood up and drained the last of his tea despite its foul sweetness.

"Let's leave me out of it," he said, attempting to regain control. "I ask only because Mrs Wilby insisted to me that Janice was smitten with Chris."

Diana Downey snapped back. "You ask because you are trying to rake up dirt amongst my parishioners. I am not a fool, Mr Mullen. Being a minister of the church does not mean I do not understand the ways of the world. Far from it. I understand temptation and sin all too well. If Janice was smitten with him — and I do say if — so too were several other women in the church, I suspect. Chris brought out their mothering side. An attractive, unattached man, down on his luck, who knew how to enlist sympathy. In that sense he was a rather dangerous man as far as I was concerned. Disruptive to my flock. Even Margaret was rather taken with him, I suspect, despite the age discrepancy. I understand she had him round for supper on at least one occasion." She turned towards the door. "Anyway, that is all I am prepared to say. I really do need to get myself organised."

Mullen nodded. He was getting his marching orders, but he didn't mind. It had been one heck of a productive meeting.

* * *

Mullen was itching to make the phone call to the 'Charles' who had rung Reverend Downey, but he waited until he was back in the silence and security of his car before pulling out his mobile and punching in the memorised numbers. The phone rang for several seconds before a woman answered. "Good afternoon. CSK. How can I help you?"

'CSK' didn't ring any bells with Mullen, but it didn't matter. All that mattered was how the receptionist reacted to his question.

"Can I speak to Charles Speight, please?"

"Of course."

There was a noise confirming that he was being put through.

Mullen hesitated. Should he hang up now before anyone could reply? He had, after all, found out what he wanted to know.

By the time he had come to a decision, the phone was already ringing. It was answered immediately. "Speight," a man said. Business-like, brusque and distracted all at once.

Mullen hung up. He was breathing heavily and sweating hard. He started the engine and opened both front windows. All he needed to do now was find out where CSK were based.

* * *

Mullen pulled into CSK's car-park at 3.50 p.m. It was situated in an identikit business park on the edge of the village of Wootton, a couple of miles to the west of Boars Hill. He drove slowly around the car-park, looking out on the one hand for a specific blue Audi A4 and on the other for a free space offering him a good but discreet place from which to view it. He breathed a sigh of relief when he saw the car and pulled into a space barely ten metres away. A good day was getting better.

He had guessed that the staff wouldn't leave before four. One or two did exit the building then, but it was only after four thirty that the trickle became more substantial. It trailed off until there was another small crescendo of activity at five. After that it was just an intermittent dribble as the number of cars slowly decreased. But still Mullen remained sitting in his car, both front windows wide open to dissipate the late afternoon heat. It was six twenty-five when Charles Speight finally appeared, laptop in one hand and folders tucked under the other arm. He was wearing what looked like a linen suit over a pin-striped shirt, but no tie. He was not sweating noticeably and that alone caused Mullen a stab of jealousy. He imagined that, unlike his car, CSK's building had fully functional air-conditioning, not to mention water-coolers on every floor.

Mullen switched on the recording application he had downloaded onto his mobile earlier that afternoon. He hadn't had a chance to use it in earnest and for all he knew the pick-up might be poor, but it was worth a try. He got out of his car and walked over to the Audi. He was almost within touching distance when Speight looked up.

"Who the hell are you?" Speight might not be suffering from the heat as Mullen was, but he had evidently not had a good day.

Mullen tried a friendly smile. "I'm a friend of Chris's."

"Chris?" Speight was momentarily flummoxed.

"The guy who was fished out of the Thames the other day near Sandford."

Speight pulled open the rear door and tossed laptop and folders onto the seat. "You must think I'm an idiot. You're a journalist, aren't you?" He slammed the door and moved to open the driver's door. Mullen stepped forward and pressed his hand against it.

"I'll shout if you don't get out of the way," Speight snapped. "The security guards will come running." Mullen looked around. There wasn't another soul in the car park and only half a dozen other cars remained. As threats went, it was patently feeble.

Mullen held up his phone. "I'm turning this off. Watch!"

Speight watched. There were one or two beads of sweat on his face now.

Mullen lifted his t-Shirt. "You can check me for wiring if you want."

Speight mumbled something indistinct.

"What did Chris die of?"

Speight shivered despite the heat, but when he spoke he seemed calm. "He drowned. There was alcohol in his blood. He must had fallen in and been unable in his drunken state to get out."

"He didn't drink."

Speight laughed. "So how did the alcohol get inside him? Osmosis?"

"By force, I presume. Had he been beaten? Were there signs he'd been restrained? There must have been marks on his wrists or bruising round the mouth where a whisky bottle had been forced in. Or something!" Mullen could hear the desperation in his own voice.

"Of course there weren't," Speight snapped. "I would have noticed. How many years do you think I've been doing this?" Speight rubbed an arm across his forehead.

"Look," he continued, "the guy must have had a relapse. Gone on a bender and fallen in the river. He wouldn't be the first and he won't be the last."

Mullen felt the day getting less good. He didn't want to, but he was finding Speight pretty convincing. He tried a wild change of attack. "Tell me about Janice Atkinson's death."

"What?" There was alarm in Speight's voice.

"Supposedly she got killed in a hit and run."

"Supposedly? There was nothing supposed about it. She got hit by a car. Her head impacted on the edge of the pavement — it was her left temple if you want to know — and she died soon afterwards. By the time the ambulance got there, she had stopped breathing and the paramedics were unable to bring her back."

"What bruising or other damage was there to her body?"

"Look, matey, I've told you more than I should have." Speight had recovered his confidence. "If you don't let me go home right now, I'll report you to the police. There's an automatic car registration system here, you know. You will be easy to track."

"You'll give Detective Inspector Dorkin a ring will you?"

The mention of Dorkin had a remarkable effect on Speight. His mouth gaped and he stared at Mullen in alarm.

"Pals are you?" Mullen said, confident that he was back in charge of the situation. "Only you didn't seem so pleased to see him the other night in the Cape of Good Hope."

Speight licked his lips and looked around helplessly. "I don't know what you mean."

Mullen smiled. His right hand was still on Speight's door, preventing him from getting into his car. His left hand, however, had retrieved his mobile from his pocket and powered it on again.

"Here, if you like I can show you a photo." It was a bluff, but Mullen doubted that Speight would call it.

"Or perhaps you'd prefer to see this one," he said, and he turned the phone so Speight could see it.

"What the devil?"

"It's you and a woman. Don't you remember you bumped into her at the bus-stop on the way home? Very chatty and smiley. I've got two or three others."

"Look, what's your game?"

"On the surface they are innocent enough I admit. A casual meeting with a young woman from the office — or maybe she's from the dentist's surgery?" Mullen paused. He could see he had scored a direct hit with that one. "Except that if an anonymous friend were to send those to your wife and suggest that you were having an affair with her, I guess it might sow seeds of doubt in her mind."

"That's blackmail." Speight's anxiety was palpable. "And it's not true."

"And you're not telling me the truth are you? Fragments of it maybe, but not the truth, the whole truth and nothing but the truth. So I'm just doing what I have to do in order to find out exactly how it was that Chris and Janice died. If you're straight with me, I'll delete the photographs from my phone here and now and you'll never hear from me again. And nor will your wife. That's a promise."

Speight looked at him. Mullen reckoned that under the suntan he had to be as white as a sheet. "I've not lied." It was the whine of a cowed dog. Mullen knew he had got Speight where he wanted him.

"I wonder what the Reverend Diana Downey would call it?" Mullen saw the surprise on Speight's face. "You do know Diana, don't you Dr Speight? Chris went to her church. So did Janice. I expect you know that too. Rather a lot of coincidences if you ask me." He paused, but only to see the effect of his words on Speight. Then he plunged on. "I expect your friend Diana would talk about sins of commission and sins of omission. But it's the sins of omission I'm interested in, Charles. What have you omitted? What is it you're not saying? Or maybe I should ask what it was that you and Dorkin were talking about in the Cape of Good Hope before you flew out of there like a bat out of hell?"

"I need to sit down."

Mullen considered this. The fact was that Speight didn't look anxious any more. He looked scared shitless. "Keys?" Mullen held out his hand, took the electronic key from Speight and then allowed him to sink into the driver's seat. Mullen stood and waited, wedging the door wide open with his body and ready to move fast if Speight did anything unexpectedly stupid.

"Rohypnol," he whispered at last.

"What?"

"It's a date-rape drug."

"I know that."

"Janice had it in her bloodstream."

"Are you saying she had been raped?"

"No. Not at all. Obviously when I discovered the drug in her system, I checked. There was no sign of recent sexual activity at all."

"Was there alcohol in her system?" Mullen's mind was starting to go to places where he really didn't want it to. But he had to ask.

"Not a lot. Maybe a large glass of wine."

"But enough to make her extremely unsteady when combined with rohypnol?" You didn't have to be a forensic pathologist to know that alcohol and rohypnol were a devastating mix.

He nodded.

"Anything else?"

Speight twitched; his left shoulder moved up and down as if controlled by a puppeteer's string. He licked his lips. "The . . . er . . . the photos on your phone?" Clearly he didn't expect Mullen to stick to his word.

But Mullen had to live with himself. Deception and lying might sometimes be necessary, but that didn't mean he felt good doing them. Without a word he bent down and deleted them one by one, right in front of Speight.

"Thank you."

Mullen handed him his key and for a few moments their eyes met and held.

"Actually . . ." There was a long pause as Speight assembled his thoughts. Mullen waited, barely daring to breathe. "Actually, there's something else I want to tell you—"

"Have a good evening, Charles!" Speight turned guiltily. A man in sunglasses was standing by a red VW convertible halfway across the car park. Speight waved from his seat and then watched until the car had disappeared from view. Only then did he turn back to Mullen, as if he was afraid the man might somehow overhear what he was about to say.

"Chris had rohypnol in his system too."

The comment came as a shot of electricity arcing across Mullen's system. He opened his mouth to say something, but nothing came out. Both brain and tongue had tripped their fuse switches.

But Speight didn't need any prompting to say more. Now that he had started, he had to get it finished.

"You see," he continued, "there wasn't actually that much alcohol in Chris's system. Enough to get him tipsy, but hardly a roaring-drunk amount. At the time I thought it was a little odd that he should fall into the river and drown. But given his lifestyle . . ." Speight ground to a halt.

Mullen felt a surge of anger. "Because he was a homeless rough sleeper, what did it matter? Right?" Mullen's decibel count was rising dramatically. "Chris wasn't important enough for you to look any closer into his death." He felt like grabbing Speight by the lapels and shaking him till his prejudices rattled.

Speight swallowed; his Adam's apple bobbing furiously in his throat. But he carried on determinedly with his account. "Like anyone, I have to prioritise what I do and don't do. But the fact is that when I had examined Janice's body and realised that there was both alcohol and rohypnol in her, it got me thinking again about Chris. So I took some hairs from his head and found traces of exactly the same type of rohypnol in it too."

"So when you met Dorkin the other night—"

"I told him what I had discovered. He was furious and started asking me what sort of pathologist I was to have missed it in the first place. He started making insinuations about my competence, which I didn't take kindly to. I take great pride in my work, but in the circumstances there had been no good reason to check for rohypnol in Chris. So I pointed out to him that the fact that I had revisited my findings on Chris and thereby located the drug in him was actually a mark of my extreme competence."

"And what did Dorkin say?"

Speight wiped his forehead again. "He was damned rude. So I just walked out. I don't have to put up with stuff like that from people like Dorkin."

Mullen nodded as if he agreed. But actually he didn't. As far as he was concerned, Dorkin had every right to throw a tantrum at Speight. The pathologist seemed to him to have been seriously at fault. End of discussion.

"All of this is off the record. Dorkin won't like it if he discovers that I've been talking out of school."

Mullen smiled at the expression. Out of school. How old school was that! But he saw no reason to make life difficult for Speight. Nor indeed did he want to draw Dorkin's attention to his own investigations. "Sure," he said. "But I've just one more question if that's OK?"

Speight exhaled. "If you must."

"If you didn't initially look for rohypnol in Chris, why did you do so in Janice?"

Speight scratched at his neck as he considered this. "Well, Dorkin told me he had a witness who had seen Janice walking rather unsteadily over Magdalen Bridge. So when I discovered that there wasn't enough alcohol in her system to justify such unsteadiness, I looked around for other reasons."

"Thanks." Mullen stepped back and finally allowed Speight to shut his door. The pathologist needed no further prompting and within seconds he was exiting the car park as if the hounds of hell were on his tail. Mullen watched him go and wondered. He wasn't sure he trusted Speight, but his story did pretty much hang together. As for what he had said about rohypnol; that really was a game-changer.

* * *

The departure of Speight coincided with the return of Mullen's headache. It had been nagging away gently throughout his long wait in the car, but now it had gained momentum and was banging away like a steam hammer. Mullen was also extremely thirsty, the consequence of having only half a small bottle of water to drink in the simmering heat. His back was complaining too, so he stopped at the Co-op in Wootton to pick up a half-litre bottle of water and some Paracetamol, plus a frozen pizza because he really couldn't face cooking anything more complicated that evening. He took three tablets, drained the bottle of water and then headed for Boars Hill.

But when he arrived back at the Cedars, he did not find the peace he craved. There were two cars pulled up in his drive. The red Punto he recognised, but the silver Rav 4 he didn't. There was no sign of the occupants. He eased himself out of his vehicle and extricated the pizza from the back seat and the empty plastic bottle from the floor.

"Ah! There you are." Becca Baines' voice boomed out. She and Rose Wilby appeared from around the back of the house and advanced towards him. "About time too. We're dying of thirst and pretty blooming hungry. But at least we had a chance to talk about you behind your back."

She laughed and pecked him on the cheek. It was, Mullen supposed, her way of telling Rose to 'Hands off!'

"Well, nice to see you both,' he said, though that wasn't entirely true. Maybe one of them, just to show him a bit of sympathy, but both of them, without warning? Apart from anything else and based on the little he knew of them, he wasn't at all sure they would hit it off. Besides, standing there with a pizza in one hand and a plastic bottle in the other, he felt as if he had been caught with his trousers down, the archetypical man incapable of cooking anything more advanced than something straight out of the freezer.

"Sorry, this isn't very fair of us turning up without warning." Rose Wilby's approach was altogether more polite and sympathetic. She patted him briefly on the forearm.

Becca laughed. It was the sort of laugh the word 'fruity' was designed for. Mullen shivered with lust. It was no wonder that men like Paul — and he — were drawn to her. "Two women on his doorstep!" Becca was squealing now. "He probably reckons he's died and gone to heaven."

Mullen tossed his house keys to her. "Let yourselves in. I just need to water the tomatoes. I could do with a cup of tea," he added. "But there's some white wine in the fridge if you want it." And he headed round the back of the house in search of a few moments of peace.

As he began to fill the watering can from the rain butt by the greenhouse, he became aware that Rose Wilby had followed him. She stood silently a couple of metres away, watching. Only when the can was full and he was turning the tap off did she speak.

"Are you and Becca an item?"

"No." He tried to sound very firm.

"I got the impression from her that you were."

"Well we definitely are not. I barely know her. And I've certainly not slept with her."

"Would you like to?"

"Jesus!" The watering can was overflowing. He turned the tap off. "Sorry! That probably offends you."

"Don't worry. It's none of my business anyway."

Mullen didn't reply. Instead he went inside the greenhouse and watered round the grow bags. His headache had abated a bit, but that was all. He really did just want some peace and quiet on his own. Apart from anything else, he needed to think.

"Actually," she said as he left the protection of the greenhouse, "I've no intention of spoiling your evening with Becca. I just want to say what I've got to say and then I'll be gone."

She moved away to the shelter of the wall, into the shade and — more pertinently Mullen thought — out of sight of Becca who was singing ostentatiously in the kitchen. "We can't pay you any more money. So as far I am concerned, the job is complete."

Mullen looked at her, trying to read her. "I'm not expecting any more money, not at the moment."

"People have gone cool. They think it was a waste of their money when the police are free and much better resourced that you can be on your own. They blame Janice for persuading them to take you on. They say she was soft on you, which was the reason she was so keen to hire you."

"I got the impression you were pretty keen to hire me too."

She didn't deny it. She didn't say anything, but Mullen had already worked out that lying wasn't something she would readily resort to.

He pressed on. "I'm making progress you know."

She shrugged. "Even so." She turned and started walking away. Mullen followed her to her car.

He let her get in. "I thought you wanted to know the truth?"

"What is truth? It's not going to make a difference, is it? Whether you find out exactly what happened or not, he'll remain dead."

"Did you love him, Rose?" It was the obvious question and he already knew the answer to it because why else would she have tears in her eyes?

But she wouldn't admit it with words. She leant over and opened a large leather bag that was lying on the passenger seat. She pulled a book out and handed it over to him. "I promised to lend this to you," she said. "I would like it back, but only when you've read it. Come round and we can talk about it and I'll even cook you a frozen pizza."

Mullen took the book — The Lion, the Witch and the Wardrobe — and felt a pang of something, a mixture of regret for himself and pity for her. He knew that he ought to ask her to stay. But instead he stepped back, closed the car door and watched her depart. Then he went inside to look for Becca Baines.

* * *

"You certainly know how to give a girl a good time."

Becca Baines and Mullen were sharing the pizza he had bought, accompanied by some rather tired-looking salad and a tin of mixed beans. He was drinking tea, while she had taken him at his word and opened some white wine.

"Rose didn't seem very happy." Becca was clearly determined to chat.

Mullen would have preferred to eat in silence, but he guessed he would have to say something. "Maybe not."

"I think she fancies you."

"I don't think so."

"She does."

Mullen stuffed a piece of pizza in his mouth.

"Would you like me to stay over tonight?"

Mullen looked across at her. "No."

She raised her eyes archly. "Well that's me told."

"I've only met you twice."

"And I've only put you to bed once." She drained the last of her wine and filled her glass again. "I just hope I don't get breathalysed on the way home."

Mullen shrugged and caved in. "You can use a spare bed if you want. But you'll have to make it up yourself."

She smiled and took another sip. "So gracious you are, Mr Mullen."

Mullen reached over and poured himself half a glass. He doubted it would do him any good as far as his (temporarily muted) headache was concerned, but he didn't see why she should drink the whole bottle. Besides she almost certainly wasn't going to like what he was about to ask her. He took a swig and swallowed. "Are you still seeing Paul Atkinson?"

"Would you be jealous if I was?"

Mullen swore and placed his glass on the table with great care. Part of him wanted to hurl it across the room to show her his frustration. Why did she have to turn everything into a joke? "It's not about me," he snapped. "Janice is dead. She asked me to help her and now she is dead. So I will ask the question again and hope for a sensible answer. Are you still seeing Paul Atkinson? Because if you are, then you must be a lot more stupid than you look."

"Janice's death was an accident, wasn't it?" Becca had sobered up and gotten serious all in a moment. "It was a hit and run, wasn't it? An accident pure and simple. The only issue being that the driver didn't stop."

"It was not an accident. It was deliberate."

"How can you possibly know that? I've read the reports on the BBC and Oxford Mail websites."

"Trust me. I'm a private investigator. I dig around and I find things out."

For the first time in their short acquaintance, Mullen saw alarm in Becca's eyes. Her skin had turned a sickly white. "How?" she said. "How——?" That was as far as she could get with her question.

"I've found a witness," he said. "It was deliberate. And I've also learnt that Janice had had her drink spiked with something which would have made her very unsteady on her feet."

Becca Baines stared at him for several seconds. She shuddered. "You're serious!" There was the beginning of panic in her voice.

Mullen pressed on. "If I was the police and I thought Janice's death was murder, then my suspicions would be directed first at Paul as her husband and then you as his lover."

She shook her head from side to side. "But I didn't."

"Have you got an alibi?"

She looked up. Her face was a battlefield. "An alibi?"

"I can vouch that you had supper with me in the Fox. There will be people who will remember us. I can tell the police that you were with me until about nine thirty, but the problem is that she wasn't killed until ten p.m. and of course from Boars Hill to the Iffley Road at that time of night doesn't take long in a car."

"Hey, you've certainly thought it through haven't you!" She spat the words out. "But there would be a dent on my car if I'd run her down. And I know for a fact that there isn't."

"For all the police know, you stole a car and then set fire to it afterwards."

Her mouth opened, but that was all.

They both fell silent. Mullen drank the rest of his wine. He needed it. Becca began to run her fingers through her hair — as if it was a wig and she was testing how well attached it was to her skull. Eventually she stopped and leaned forward. "Doug, you surely don't think I killed Janice do you?"

Mullen didn't answer at first. The grandfather clock in the hall chimed eight o'clock. It felt like midnight and his headache had returned.

"Tell me you don't!"

"I really don't know what to think, Becca."

She stood up suddenly, knocking over her glass as she did so. "I'll be off then. The last thing you want is a murderer in your precious house." She stamped across the kitchen towards the hall.

"You've drunk too much to be driving," he called after her.

"You sound like my mother, Mullen." She hurled the taunt over her shoulder, but didn't look back. Mullen didn't follow her. Instead he emptied what was left of the wine into his glass and listened: to her car door slamming shut, to the engine bursting into life and to the wheels shooting gravel out behind them. Then silence descended and with it came a strange mixture of relief and sadness.

* * *

It was only when she had put her mother to bed just before ten o'clock that Doreen Rankin allowed herself the stiff gin and tonic she had been thinking about all evening. Normally she settled down in front of the BBC news with a mug of tea, but these were not normal circumstances and for once the stories of doom, gloom and violence failed to engage her. She killed the TV with a savage curse, pushed herself up from the sofa and hobbled over to the bookshelf.

Her right hand homed in on one of her favourite books, about the Pre-Raphaelites. She took it over to the table where the two of them always ate and opened it up. It fell open where she knew it would — Ophelia floating face-upwards in the river, singing with apparent serenity shortly before she was dragged down to her doom. 'Her clothes spread wide,' as Shakespeare recorded it, 'her garments, heavy with their drink, pull'd the poor wretch from her melodious lay to muddy death.' Rankin mouthed the words as she had mouthed them so often before, but neither Shakespeare's words nor Millais's painting held her as they usually did.

What dragged at her like Ophelia's garments was the innocuous-looking brown envelope lying between the pages of the book and the three incriminating photographs which she knew lay inside it. She wished she had destroyed them as she had promised Paul she would. If she had done that, she could have pretended to herself that they had never existed — or at least that she had never known anything about them. If only!

She slipped her right hand inside the envelope and pulled out the photographs. They looked no better after a good slug of alcohol than they had when she had so unsuspectingly opened them in the office. She could destroy them now, she told herself. It wasn't too late. She didn't have a shredder here at home and there was no open fire or wood-burner in their twenty-first century apartment, but a pair of her mother's pinking shears would quickly reduce them to a pile of indecipherable and unrecoverable paper shreds. Except that she had seen on some TV drama that there were people who were experts at putting shredded paper back together. She guessed it was a bit like doing a jigsaw puzzle, but without a picture to guide you.

There was a noise — or rather a series of noises all too familiar to Doreen Rankin: a heavy thump as her mother swung herself heavily out of bed, a shuffling of feet, the bang of a door. It was the first of her mother's frequent nocturnal trips. She took another couple of sips of her gin and tonic and listened, waiting for the noises that would signal that her mother had returned to her bed. She was convinced that sooner or later she would fall and crack her skull on a piece of furniture or snap her hip.

She sipped again at her glass and realised there was only ice at the bottom of it. She poured herself another drink, with a bit more gin this time, and dropped in some extra ice as compensation. She returned to the sofa, glass in one hand and photographs in the other, and slumped down. She took a swig and belched.

Alcohol was supposed to confuse and befuddle the mind. But that wasn't how it felt to Doreen Rankin. Quite the opposite. Things were becoming clearer with every mouthful. She couldn't possibly destroy the photographs. They were evidence. She ought to give them to the police. Except that doing so would be a second betrayal of Paul. Unless of course he had killed Janice, in which case helping the police was her duty. But having an affair did not make Paul Atkinson a killer. He was a charmer, yes. Doreen was pretty darned sure that he had cheated on his wife several times on business trips to Europe and the States. But that didn't mean he would have killed his wife if she had found out. What would have been the point? To judge from the way he treated her and the angry phone calls she herself had received from Janice, they weren't exactly a match made in heaven.

She took another sip and discovered she was down to the ice again. It was amazing how quickly a nice G & T disappeared. She eased herself up, made her way over to the table again and poured herself another refill. This was the last one tonight, she promised herself. Definitely the last. She took a gulp and looked again at one of the photographs. It was the one where Paul had his hand on the woman's fat bottom and she was whispering something in his ear. Doreen picked up the next one. It was, she now realised, taken almost immediately after the first (Paul's hand was still on the bitch's bottom), only in this shot Paul's face was visible and there was a terrible leering grin spread right across it. She must have been whispering something quite disgusting into his ear. Doreen took another gulp from her glass and felt the anger rise. It was the woman's fault! Paul was an attractive but weak man, easy prey for the unscrupulous woman. She knew that. She had always known that. Well, she wasn't going play into the bitch's hands. She was going to find the pinking shears and go to work on the photographs. And when she had got a nice pile of shredded paper, she'd burn them just to be sure. And later on, in a few days' time, when Paul had recovered from Janice's death, she would tell him what she had done. He would be so pleased.

Doreen stood up and moved unsteadily over to the fireplace. She took the lid off a small Chinese jar and extricated a packet of cigarettes and a box of matches. She lit up and blew a wreath of smoke up towards the ceiling, watching it as it expanded and then disappeared. Her mother wouldn't approve, but she didn't care. What harm could a cigarette or two do?

Chapter 7

Mullen slept soundly that night. The day had sucked the energy out of him and although he went to bed with the events and discoveries of the last twelve hours spinning in his head, his body's need for rest and recuperation had the final say. He woke once to go to the toilet, but apart from that he was conscious of nothing until his mobile phone woke him. He rolled over, picked it up and checked the caller display; 'Unknown.' Most likely some wretched cold caller. He killed the call.

He had barely lain back down before his mobile rang again. The same 'Unknown' was displayed. He groaned. His gut reaction was to ignore the call again and turn his mobile off, but something stopped him. Did these automated dialling systems dial you again immediately? He thought not. More likely they did so the next day or the next week. Which meant, he realised, that this was very likely a human being calling, not a salesperson. Hiding your number when you made a call was easy enough to do if you knew how. The phone continued to ring and Mullen reluctantly swung his legs over the side of the mattress and sat up. He pressed the answer icon, lifted the mobile to his ear and listened. There was silence, except for the muffled sound of someone breathing.

"Who is it?"

"Is that the Good Samaritan?"

"What?" Even if Mullen hadn't been half asleep, the reference would have confused him.

"It's a dangerous role."

This time Mullen said nothing. He knew when someone was threatening him. He knew too — or thought he did — that if he kept quiet and avoided rising to the bait then the chances were that the caller would say more.

"Did you hear me?" There was a crack of irritation in the voice, even though it sounded artificial. Mullen was reminded of Stephen Hawking.

"Are you trying to frighten me?"

"It's not you who should be frightened. It's your friends."

It was like being kicked in the stomach. Mullen felt the bile rise and tasted the bitterness in his throat. He opened his mouth and forced himself to say something.

"What do you mean?" Keep him talking, he told himself. And listen, Mullen, really listen — to his stupid voice, to what he says and how he says it, for any background noise.

"Unless you stop," the man continued, "one of your friends will pay the price."

And then the line went dead.

* * *

By the time Mullen had showered, dressed in clean clothes, eaten some muesli and downed a mug of black coffee, he felt almost ready to face the day. His headache of the night before was a distant memory, though anxiety was beating its own drum inside his head.

Should he take the phone call seriously? The answer was surely 'yes.' Should he contact the police about it? Of course he should. Otherwise, if something did happen to one of his friends, he would never forgive himself. Would DI Dorkin and DS Fargo take him seriously? The answer to that question was less certain.

Even so, Mullen made the call and after an argument with the person on the end of the line he got transferred to Dorkin. Except that the person who answered certainly wasn't Dorkin, not unless he had had a sex-change or a nasty cricketing accident.

"Your name, sir?" the woman said in a flat Brummie accent.

"Doug Mullen. I need to speak to DI Dorkin."

There was a pause before she replied.

"I'm afraid he's out. I'm Detective Constable Ashe. Perhaps I can help."

"Is DS Fargo there?"

"He's out too."

"I need to speak to one of them."

"About what?"

"About two murders and an anonymous phone call."

"I see."

There was another pause. Mullen wondered if she was getting advice or merely making him wait for the sake of it. Then: "They'll be in touch shortly." And she put the phone down before he could argue or complain.

Mullen shrugged and leant back in the large Windsor chair he had adopted as his own. "And pigs will fly," he said to the empty kitchen.

Mullen was wrong. 'Shortly' turned out to be a lot sooner than he could possibly have expected. He had only just gone upstairs and brushed his teeth when a banging at the door summoned him back downstairs.

"Hello, again!" The sour smile and gravelly greeting belonged to Dorkin. Behind him, Fargo loomed silent and surly. He seemed to be larger every time they met. "I'd like a little chat," Dorkin continued, pushing inside. Fargo followed and Mullen, shutting the door, couldn't help but notice that there were two uniformed officers standing in the drive, one of whom headed off round the side of the house. Were they out there in case he did a runner? It wasn't a good sign.

He walked back through to the kitchen where Dorkin was making himself comfortable in Mullen's favourite chair, while Fargo stood against the wall, arms folded and still very large.

"I've just been trying to get hold of you on the phone," Mullen said.

Dorkin's eyebrows rose minimally. "Oh yeah?"

"I've had an anonymous phone call this morning. Someone warned me they would hurt one of my friends if I didn't stop my investigation."

"Did they now?" Dorkin rubbed his chin. "Can I see your mobile? I assume they rang you on your mobile?"

Mullen unlocked it and passed it over. "You'll see it in the call log. 'Unknown.'"

There was a flicker of a smile on Dorkin's face. He studied Mullen's mobile for the best part of a minute, then placed it on the table. "I may need to borrow that for a while. Have you got a spare one?"

"No."

"You don't have an unregistered, pay-as-you-go one? I thought all smart private investigators kept a stock of them just in case they needed to do naughty things without being caught. For example, they might want to use one to ring up the mobile phone which is registered in their name. That way they can pretend to be an anonymous caller making untraceable threats."

Mullen stared back at the inspector. He seemed to be enjoying himself. But what the heck was going on? Why wasn't Dorkin taking him seriously?

Mullen stood up and leant forward across the table towards Dorkin. He heard Fargo tense for action, but Dorkin didn't even blink. "There's someone out there, Inspector, threatening to kill my friends. And you're sitting there like some—"

Mullen never finished his sentence because one of Fargo's huge hands had gripped him by the arm and was spinning him around as if he was a kid's top from the days when kids had proper simple toys. The next thing Mullen knew was that he had been rammed back into his chair and two hands were holding his shoulders extremely firmly.

Dorkin's smile had been replaced by a stony glare. "Shall I tell you why we aren't taking you too seriously, Mullen? There are two reasons. Number one, it's because you kept secret from us the fact that you and Becca Baines are pals. That you bought her a meal on Tuesday evening."

"Actually we went Dutch."

Fargo's hands tensed, digging into his shoulders even more.

"This is the woman you were spying on. You mess up her sex life and the next thing is you're dating her."

"Not dating her. She came round to give me a verbal roasting, but I was only just out of hospital and I fainted in front of her. What with her being a nurse, well it changed things."

"So you ended up in bed together?"

"No!" Mullen felt himself getting riled. "She put me to bed. She slept in a chair in the room. I think she was worried about me."

"But you must like her because you had supper with her."

"We have a shared interest."

"Like stamp collecting?"

"Like finding out who killed Janice."

"And why would she be interested in doing that?"

"Because, like me, she's probably worried that you'll try and pin it on her."

Dorkin considered this, rubbing his fingers on his forehead. Then he gave a shake of his whole body and changed tack. He felt inside his jacket and pulled out a mobile phone. He took a few seconds to find what he wanted to find, then stretched across the table and held it close to Mullen's face. "Take a look at this, sunshine."

Mullen recognised who and where the photograph had been taken almost immediately.

"Our colleague, Detective Constable Ashe, is a bit of a Facebook obsessive. Always posting her holiday photos and sharing stupid stuff she's spotted on the internet. I tell her it's bad for her. I point out that people are more important than computers. But when has any woman taken a blind bit of notice of what I say?" The wry smile was back on Dorkin's face. "But that's one of the strengths of having someone like Ashe on the team. She thinks differently and has other ideas. Like looking to see if the Meeting Place had a Facebook page and then going through everything on it in great detail after she'd gone home and put her little boy to bed. All in her own time, bless her cotton socks. And then, amidst all the photographs up there, she finds this one."

Mullen said nothing.

"You recognise yourself, of course?"

"Of course."

"And the man you're talking to. The man with long hair."

"Of course I do." Mullen was trying to think and finding it difficult. He hadn't realised anyone had been taking any photos that evening. But of course anyone and everyone with a mobile phone can take a decent photograph in an instant nowadays and it's impossible to stop. And here he was in a photograph with Chris and Chris had got his hand on Mullen's shoulder as if they were best mates. And indeed the benign smile on Mullen's face didn't gainsay that.

"There are three others actually, Muggins. And they all suggest that you and Chris got on pretty well."

Muggins! A flash flood of anger caused Mullen to grip the arms of the chair. If he lost control, it would be just the excuse Dorkin needed. Even so, when Mullen did finally speak, he did so more sharply and louder than he had intended. "It's my job to get on well with people."

"It's your job to stop people getting out of hand."

"I don't believe in bullying people. I've seen it happen in the army. My best mate was bullied and he blew his own brains out. So I try to be nice to people and I only lay down the law when people are in danger of getting out of hand. I find it works best that way."

Dorkin made a show of clapping, bringing his hands together and away again in slow motion, several times. "Bravo!" he said. Mullen pretended not to care. If there was a 'taking the piss' module in police training school, Dorkin had clearly passed with distinction.

"Are you gay, Mullen?"

Mullen said nothing.

"Chris was."

There was more silence. The only significant noise was the heavy breathing of Fargo. He could sense the sergeant tensing behind him, waiting for the explosion that Dorkin was trying to detonate.

"Who told you that?" Mullen knew he had to wrest the initiative back from the inspector. There was nothing to be gained by lying down and letting Dorkin stamp all over him.

"Wouldn't you like to know!" There was the smile again.

Mullen stretched his arms. He felt Fargo's hands alight ever so briefly on his shoulders in warning. He tried to think. Dorkin was trying to provoke a reaction. There were gays at the Meeting Place, of course there were. But Mullen doubted very much if Chris had been one of them. On the contrary, he had always seemed interested in the opposite sex, whether it was the waif-like Mel or a couple of the female punters who were always up for a nice flirt and maybe a lot more.

"I would, as it happens. But obviously you're not going to tell me."

"What were you two talking about in those photos then?"

Mullen knew it was easier — and safer — to tell the truth. Besides, he wasn't sure how good he was at making things up on the spot. The chances were that Dorkin already had some idea about the conversation. Maybe someone had overheard some of it and informed the police. Kevin Branston or Mel or one of the punters.

"Chris was a bit on edge," he started. "So a bit like Sergeant Fargo here, I put my hand on his shoulder to calm him down." Mullen paused.

Dorkin looked at Fargo and nodded his head, which as far as Mullen was concerned could have meant anything. Grab him. Give him a slap to help his memory. Something like that. Fortunately Fargo didn't interpret it that way. Instead he padded around the table and settled himself in front of the sink unit, close to Dorkin and in full view of Mullen.

"We need a bit more detail than that, Doug."

"He didn't say what it was about. It was only the third time I'd come across him at the Meeting Place and I'd not had any trouble from him previously. But that night he was on edge. Of course it was a special evening, when supporters of the project had been invited to come and see how it all worked and meet people. Maybe that had got to him. Or maybe it was something more personal. Anyway one of the other guys said something — I didn't hear what — and Chris started to get aggressive with him. He was only a couple of metres away from me, so I stepped over to calm him down. I think that was when I put my hand on his shoulder. In retrospect it was a bit of a risk to take. He might have turned on me, but at the time it seemed to be the quickest and best way to kill off any trouble. With there being so many visitors, Kevin Branston had warned me not to let anything develop. Anyway that was what I did and it worked."

Dorkin sucked at his teeth as if he had got a piece of food stuck in them. "So in the other photos of you and him talking, are you telling me that you can't remember what you and he said? Didn't you ask him what the problem was?"

"I asked him if he wanted to talk about it."

Dorkin stared back at Mullen. "You're a ruddy counsellor too are you now?"

"Not a very good one." Mullen felt light-headed, as if he had consumed too much alcohol on an empty stomach. "Chris just changed the subject. He started asking me about the World Cup."

* * *

As soon as Dorkin and his colleagues had driven away, Mullen got out his laptop. If Detective Constable Ashe could interrogate Facebook, then so could he.

It didn't take long to find the photos of himself and Chris. It had been right at the beginning of the evening. There was already quite a scrum of punters and Chris had been in an awkward mood. Not that there had been any real trouble from him. That had come from Alec and John who had ended up fighting in the main hall — fortunately before the guests had arrived. Less fortunately Alec had ended up with a broken nose. The last thing Branston had wanted that evening was trouble, so after ordering John off the premises he had insisted Mullen drive Alec straight up to Accident and Emergency and stay with him until he had been dealt with. Two hours later Mullen had returned to the Meeting Place to discover the food and guests had all disappeared, leaving behind them a blocked toilet which he ended up having to sort out.

Mullen began to flick quickly through the rest of the album, curious to see what he had missed. But after only six photos he lifted his finger and stopped. On the screen in front of him was the Reverend Diana Downey. She stood out with her dog collar and rather flimsy clothing and was quite clearly attracting a lot of attention from the men there. Mullen scratched at his head. It wasn't, as soon as he thought about it, so surprising that she should be there. You would expect a place like that to attract the support of churches. And it offered a more innocent explanation of why Kevin Branston had been visiting the Reverend Downey the other day. (Though it didn't, Mullen reckoned, entirely explain Branston's rather furtive exit from the vicarage. Or had he been imagining it?)

If Downey was there, had other people from St Mark's church also come along to see how their money was being spent? As Mullen continued with a more careful trawl through the album, he soon got some answers. Downey appeared in several of them, always talking to a different person. Whoever it was who had been clicking away had been taken with her too. Mullen spotted Derek Stanley with his tell-tale goatee, talking to some of the regular punters. In another, more surprisingly, was Margaret Wilby, immaculately dressed in navy blue and white and talking to the student Mel and the punter who was always hanging around her. Was Wilby on some church committee and coming along in her official capacity? There were a couple of other faces that Mullen recognised from the church service, but otherwise nothing until he came across a picture that stopped his forefinger dead. In the centre, with his back to the camera, was Chris. The fact that his face was turned away didn't mean he wasn't easy to identify with his olive green t-shirt and camouflage trousers. Talking to him was Janice Atkinson, arm in arm with her husband Paul, and next to them stood Derek Stanley, listening intently. There was someone beyond Stanley — but all that was visible of him or her was a raised glass, a hand and a white sleeve. Was it Diana Downey? Mullen flicked to the next photograph in case it should reveal more. It didn't. It contained mostly punters, except for the distinctive figure of Margaret Wilby, lips pursed as if the wine in her glass didn't come up to scratch. Or maybe she thoroughly disapproved of the whole business. Mullen flicked on again, but realised he was back at the beginning with photos of the outside of the building bedecked with a long banner wishing everyone 'Welcome to our Open Evening.'

He went back to the shot he was really interested in and dwelt on it for some time until he had all the details registered in his brain. He prided himself on what he could store away; it wasn't exactly a photographic memory, but it was pretty good nevertheless.

After that he made himself a cup of tea and sat down again with a pad and pen. He revisited every photo, this time making a note of everyone he recognised from the church, the people they appeared to be talking to (in so far as he recognised them) and the photograph number concerned.

By the time he had got to the end, his tea, barely touched, was cold, but he drank it anyway, not caring, because he had more important things to worry about.

Such as where was Kevin Branston in all the photographs? The answer was nowhere. Did that mean he was the photographer? The only problem with that theory, Mullen told himself, was that it didn't entirely fit with what he had observed of the man. Branston worked hard. He wasn't averse to doing some of the background and menial work when required, but he wasn't a man who avoided the limelight either. It was unquestionably odd that there wasn't even a single photo of him in the Facebook album. He had got himself into the Oxford Mail the day after that open evening — a flattering photograph and an article that painted him and his project in glowing colours.

And what was he to make of Paul and Janice Atkinson? No sign of marital disharmony there. But then what did he expect? If you're having an affair and your marriage is on the verge of going down the pan, that doesn't mean you don't put on shows of unity. But Janice's arm was tucked through Paul's and there was a broad smile on her face;

either it was a very brave bit of play-acting or she didn't at that stage have a clue about his affair. Except that this took place only a week or so before she had contacted Mullen and hired him to track her husband.

And then there was Margaret Wilby, glaring out of the background as if this was the last place on earth she wanted to be. Why was she there if that was the case? Was she there out of duty, under sufferance? Or had there been some falling out with someone earlier that evening?

Mullen clicked the screen of his laptop down and stood up. He felt confused and frustrated, not just with the overload of thoughts, but with the attitude of DI Dorkin. He clearly thought that the anonymous threatening call which Mullen had told them about was fiction, whereas Mullen could still hear the voice of the man in his head, telling him that one of his friends would pay the price. What did he mean by that? Presumably that he was prepared to kill again if Mullen didn't give up his investigation. Who were the friends he was threatening? He had only been in the area a few months and there were few (if any) people he could genuinely call friends. Rose? Possibly. Becca? He guessed so. Kevin Branston? Mel or Brian or Jean or any of the other volunteers at the Meeting Place? They were all nice to him and twice they had all had a drink together after the evening sessions. What about Pavel from the Iffley Road flats? Ultimately it depended on what the caller meant by 'friend.'

* * *

In the end Mullen decided he had had enough and made his way into the garden. He thought he'd check the tomato plants for water, weed the vegetable patch and tidy up generally. It would help him to switch his brain off for a while and when he had finished he would take a few photographs so that the professor could see that he was looking after the place. But he had barely got his hoe out before he heard a car pull into the drive. There was a wild attention-grabbing hooting. So whoever it was, it wasn't the police again. He straightened up and walked round the side path, carrying his hoe. It wouldn't hurt to show he was in the middle of something.

It was Becca Baines. She grinned. "Ah, it's the hired gardener." She held up two bags. "Lunch! Nice and healthy: salad and fresh rolls, plus strawberries for pudding."

Mullen realised with a start that he was pleased to see her — and also hungry. But he was puzzled that she hadn't rung first. "I might have been out," he said.

"In that case I would have eaten solo in your lovely garden and then sunbathed until it was time to go to work." She smiled. "I'm on the night shift today."

They ate at the teak garden table, half in the shade and half out. They talked easily. Or rather Becca talked while Mullen listened. Not that he minded. She was good, lively company. Eventually they finished and he went inside to make them coffee. She followed with the debris of lunch.

"You seem distracted," she said as she put the leftovers in the fridge.

"Sorry."

"Well are you going to tell me about it or do I have to apply Chinese burns to extract the information?"

So Mullen started to talk. About Chris, about Janice, about the police's questioning that morning and about what he had seen on Facebook. The only thing he didn't mention was the anonymous caller.

"Show me," she said. So he did.

He took her through each photograph, telling her who he knew in each one. She was silent now, murmuring occasionally, sipping her coffee, taking it all in. When he got to the end, he turned and looked at her. "Any thoughts?"

"There are more shots of your glamorous vicar friend than anyone," she said.

"Yes."

"And no wedding ring on her finger."

"No."

"Is she gay?"

"I don't know."

"I bet she isn't." Becca had taken over the laptop. She moved back to one of the photographs of Diana Downey, mouth open, laughing, surrounded by punters. "Look at her. She likes to be the centre of male attention. A bit of a prick-teaser, if you ask me. Hiding behind her clerical robes."

Mullen almost pointed out that she didn't seem to wear 'clerical' clothes even in church, but managed not to.

"Who took the photos?" Becca said.

"Sorry?" Mullen was taken off guard by the change of direction. "I don't know."

"A man, I bet. Probably fancies her something rotten."

It was a light bulb in the brain moment for Mullen. Of course! It was so obvious. Kevin Branston! It all made sense. Branston was conspicuously absent from the photographs, so the chances were that it was him taking the photos. And it was Branston who had been leaving Diana Downey's house in something of a hurry before Mullen's own appointment with her. He was probably in charge of the Facebook account too, making sure there were plenty of photos of their open evening on display — not to mention Reverend Downey in all her glamour. He was besotted with her. The question was: did she feel the same way about him?

"Well?" Becca was looking at him impatiently. "What's going on in that tiny little brain of yours? Because I can hear the cogs clicking, albeit rather slowly."

Mullen explained. Becca listened with a brow so furrowed it might have been a freshly ploughed field. He thought he found her even more attractive when she was in serious mode. When he had finished, he waited for her to respond. He needed help and he reckoned that she —

being a woman and detached — might be the person to provide it.

"I suppose the question is: does the vicar getting up to a bit of hanky-panky with your boss have any relevance to the two deaths?"

"It's possible, I suppose. If someone was trying to blackmail them, maybe . . ." Mullen dribbled to a halt. Just putting his thinking into words seemed to highlight how flimsy it was.

Becca was looking at him inscrutably. "You don't seem very certain."

"No." He scratched his head. "Well, these days it wouldn't be the end of the world if such a relationship came to light would it?"

"Is Kevin Branston married?"

Mullen felt very stupid. He hadn't thought of that. But he knew the answer to her question. "He wears a wedding ring."

"So put yourself in the Reverend's shoes. She's fallen for a married guy. They are sleeping together. Every Sunday she stands up in the pulpit and preaches the ten commandments and all that jazz. Then Chris and Janice find out and they decide to apply a bit of blackmail. 'Woman Vicar is a Marriage Wrecker!' You can imagine the headlines in the Daily Trash, can't you? So Reverend Downey tells Kevin it's all over and she tells him why. But Kevin is obsessed with her. No way is he going to let her finish with him. He's going to sort the two of them out permanently. So he arranges two very different 'accidents.' Maybe he doesn't even tell Diana."

She downed the last of her coffee and put her mug on the side. "Well?"

"OK," Mullen said. "You've made a good case. But where's the hard evidence?"

"You're the private eye, buster."

* * *

Mullen's intention had been to get to the Meeting Place early and in some way or other confront Kevin Branston. He hadn't worked out the details in his head when he left Boars Hill. But the road to hell is paved with good intentions, as the saying goes, especially on the Oxford ring road system on a Friday, when the rush hour begins midway through the afternoon and lasts forever — or so it seemed to Mullen as he sat fuming in his car on the slow drag towards the Heyford Hill roundabout.

So Mullen actually arrived five minutes late, which put him at an immediate disadvantage. Branston was onto him within seconds, even though he had tried to slip in unobtrusively.

"What time do you call this, Mullen?"

"Sorry, the traffic was really bad."

"The traffic is the same for everyone," Branston snapped. Mullen was tempted to argue the toss on that. Branston was within cycling distance, so of course queues of stationary vehicles weren't going to affect him significantly. But he merely apologised again.

"I'm really sorry, Kevin. It really was just a misjudgement. I've moved house and didn't realise quite how long it would take me. I'll allow more time next Friday."

"Good." Branston seemed to be mollified. He switched into his more normal organisational mode. "We're one down in the kitchen. So keep an eye on the food queues. Hungry people don't like to be kept waiting. And of course England are pretty much down and out of the World Cup, so who knows how that will affect people's mood."

"Sure." Mullen moved off through the scrum of people. He had noticed on the BBC website that England had crashed to their second defeat the previous night. What with everything else going on in his life, it seemed totally irrelevant. But he knew from his own brief footballing career in the army how easily passions were raised and how much it hurt when your team lost.

"See the game last night?" It was Brian. Mullen liked him. He and his wife Jean were there every Friday doing their bit. He had a pack of loo rolls under his arm. "Urgent delivery!" he laughed. And then he was gone.

It was a subdued crowd that evening. Mullen put it down partly to depression resulting from England's World Cup disaster. It had been a lovely day, the warmest of the week, and although that meant people were very happily smoking and chatting outside, everyone seemed rather flat. The only person who got excited about the food being slower than usual was a man called Terry who had diabetes and hence a very short fuse at meal times. Mullen got a roll off Jean and made him chew on it. He suspected that Terry was making the most of his condition to try and jump to the front of the queue. He wasn't having that, but equally he didn't want unnecessary trouble. He'd bring it up at the end-of-day team meeting in case there were better ways he could have handled it.

But apart from another blockage in the gents loo — this time a combination of a pair of pants and two plastic bags — it was a pretty uneventful evening. After the punters had gone and the clearing and cleaning up had been completed, the team settled down with cups of tea and debriefed.

Terry and Jean complained about the shortage of cloths and cleaning materials, but in general everyone seemed to be keen to get off home. Branston, who had been yawning intermittently through the meeting, called Mullen back as he prepared to leave.

"Hey," he said. "I understand it was you who found Chris dead in the river."

"Yeah." Mullen could hardly deny it. That sort of information was bound to come out eventually, though he was surprised. No-one else at the Meeting Place had mentioned it, which meant that it surely wasn't public knowledge. He wondered who Branston's source was.

"That's quite a coincidence," Branston continued, looking askance at Mullen. "Do you want to tell me about it?"

Mullen shook his head. "Not really. Maybe after the coroner has passed judgement."

Branston gave another yawn. His breath smelt of garlic and mints. But he hadn't finished. "It must have been quite a surprise for you."

"Looks like you need an early night," Mullen replied, trying to change the subject.

Branston yawned again. "Ten out of ten for observation, Doug." He pressed his shoulders back, flexing his arms. "Gina, my wife, wakes me up. She's always waking up and then she turns on the lights and fusses about getting cups of tea and scanning the internet on her tablet. So I wake up too and then I can't get back to sleep either."

"Can't the doctor prescribe something for her?" A thought was flitting elusively round Mullen's brain.

"Of course. And they have done. But it's a dangerous road. I don't approve myself. You can easily become dependent on them. So Gina saves them for when she's feeling desperate. As for me, I just move into the spare room when I need an uninterrupted night."

Mullen paused. He was tempted to ask what drugs the doctor had prescribed for Gina Branston, but something held him back — caution or intuition — and then the opportunity was gone.

"Anyway, we are all done here," Branston said with finality. "Time to go home." He turned off the hall lights in order to drive home his point. "See you next week, Doug."

Mullen nodded and said goodnight. His opportunity had gone, but his suspicions remained.

Chapter 8

The dream began in the usual way. He was back in the army and was opening the door into Ben's bedroom. There was a smell of joss sticks, which was strange because Ben never burned joss sticks. He was sitting at his small table. The room was dark except for where his red, blue and white angle-poise lamp cast a glaring light down onto a book over which Ben was hunched. Mullen was puzzled. He walked over to the desk to see what the book was because Ben was not a reader of books.

"Hello, mate," Ben said, turning his head. Mullen didn't dare look at him because he knew what he would see. That black hole where his mouth and nose should be. He bent down and closed the book so that he could see what it was. An animal's face stared out at him: The Lion, the Witch and the Wardrobe. Then he became aware of a ringing sound. Half awake, Mullen felt for his mobile and answered the call.

"Who's that?"

"Fitz," said a thick Glaswegian accent. "You said to ring. It's about Chris."

Mullen's somnolent brain woke up, identifying the guy to whom he had given the last of his supply of cigarettes. "Yes?"

"You promised twenty quid."

"OK. Where shall we meet?"

"There's a good café in St Giles. In half an hour."

"Half an hour? Not sure I can be there that soon."

"I'll wait outside." He hung up.

* * *

Fitz was sitting on the pavement, legs crossed, eyes cast down and a cap laid upside down in front of him. There were half a dozen coins in the bottom, but only one of them was silver.

"Fitz?"

As soon as Mullen spoke, the man leapt to his feet with surprising alacrity, scooping up hat and money as he did so.

"Thought you weren't coming."

"You know what thought did," Mullen replied, quoting something that his teacher Miss King used to say to him without ever explaining further.

"I'm hungry."

A full English breakfast was clearly part of the deal as far as Fitz was concerned. Mullen didn't mind. He ordered himself one too. It was a welcome change from Muesli. And as long as Fitz was waiting for and then eating his breakfast and drinking his tea, he was a captive audience.

"So, tell me about Chris."

"Hungry," Fitz said.

Doug shrugged and waited. Two mugs of tea were soon delivered, but Fitz remained sullen and silent. The teas were followed, with impressive speed, by two plates piled with the sort of fry-up a man would die for. Mullen dug in, pushing a fork piled high with bacon, egg, sausage and toast into his mouth. He shuddered with pleasure. He looked across at Fitz, who grunted rhythmically as he swallowed three mouthfuls of food in quick succession. At that rate, Mullen reckoned, he would be done and dusted within minutes and then out of the door. Maybe this was a mistake, another dead end up which he had been led. Fitz jerked his head up as if he had read Mullen's thoughts and gave a toothy grin.

"He was a tight bastard."

Fitz took another slug of tea from his mug and belched. Mullen sipped at his tea and waited.

"Tried to borrow off me. He pretended he was skint. I was stupid enough to give him a tenner, but I never got it back."

"If he didn't have any money, why do you say he was tight?"

Fitz pushed another fork-load of food into his mouth and chewed it more slowly, maybe spinning out his pleasure. He wiped his mouth with the back of his hand and looked across at Mullen again, this time without a trace of a grin.

"I was in Costa, the one in Queen Street. Some old lady took pity on me and bought me a coffee and a sandwich. Nice old girl. She even stopped and chatted for a while and watched my things while I went to the loo. But she said she had to catch her bus, so I sat tight for a bit longer, dragging it out for as long as I could. It was raining outside. Then I saw Chris. He was coming down the circular stairs and he paused halfway down. He had a wodge of notes in his hand. He was counting them — there were twenty at least, I'd say."

"What value were the notes?" Mullen had begun to wonder if Fitz was just giving him a run for his money, making up a good story to ensure he got the promised reward. Asking about the detail seemed a better way of finding out the truth than challenging him directly.

"Twenties," Fitz said instantly. "I reckoned he must have had the best part of five hundred quid with him."

"Did you speak to him?"

"No."

"Why ever not? You could have asked for your tenner back couldn't you?"

Fitz returned to his food, shovelling in a couple more mouthfuls. Then he drained his mug and leant back in his chair. "You promised me twenty quid."

Mullen opened his wallet and removed three ten-pound notes, but he didn't hand them over. "Why didn't you speak to Chris in Costa? Or follow him outside?"

"I was going to." Fitz belched and then licked the fingers of his left hand. "I stood up and got my clobber. But there was a guy coming down the stairs a few steps behind him. I knew him — sort of. When he got to the bottom, he spotted me. He came over and said 'hello,' so I had to ask him how he was and all that stuff and by the time we'd finished Chris was out of sight."

"Who was he, this guy?"

Fitz said nothing. He had returned to his breakfast, shovelling it in as if he was in 'Cinderella' and the clock had started to strike twelve.

"Who was he?" Mullen repeated quietly, leaning forward.

Fitz picked up a final piece of toast in his fingers and wiped it around his plate, determined not to waste even a smear.

"Kevin," he said eventually. "Runs the drop-in down in Cowley. I used to go there, but I prefer to stay in town now. Gatehouse, Archway. They're better. More convenient."

"Describe him," Mullen said. Not that he needed a description of his boss at the Meeting Place, but it was a way of checking if Fitz was for real or not.

"Round face. Dark hair." Fitz chuckled. "I think he was a bit offended I'd stopped coming to his place."

"Did he speak to Chris as he came downstairs?"

Fitz shrugged and began to pull his anorak on. "Don't think so." He stood up. "I reckon I've earned my money, and more." He held out his hand.

Mullen nodded towards the counter. "See the guy there. I'm giving thirty quid to him. He'll keep it on a tab for you. It'll buy you a few good meals."

Mullen didn't get up, but he tensed himself nevertheless because it was impossible to know how Fitz would react. It would have been much easier to give Fitz the cash and let him spend it on booze or drugs, but that went against Mullen's code. "I thought that would be a good way of keeping the money safe for you," he said, trying to head off any trouble. "No-one can nick it from you when you're asleep."

Fitz didn't reply. He turned away, pushing past a student who had just entered the cafe. He was angry, but Mullen was pretty sure he'd come back when he was hungry.

* * *

Mullen didn't know Branston's address, but he knew he cycled to work on a not very flash bike, so the chances were he lived locally. A search for the name Branston on his smart phone (Mullen was gradually getting smarter in its use) came up with just two results and only one of these could possibly be Kevin: KL Branston, living in Crescent Road, Oxford. It didn't ring a bell with Mullen, whose knowledge of the city was curate's-eggish. But BT provided a convenient 'Map' link and within moments Mullen could see it was a long straggling road in Temple Cowley. He studied the surrounding streets for several seconds, imprinting the area in his brain, before stuffing his phone in his pocket and striding off down St Aldates in search of his car. He had briefly considered ringing Branston to see if he was in — he had his mobile number in case of work issues — but he had dismissed the idea almost instantly. He wanted to apply pressure and he reckoned that appearing unannounced on his doorstep would be a good way of doing that, especially if his wife was at home.

The house was stuck in the middle of a long terrace — red Victorian brick, white sash windows with peeling paint, dark blue door with cobwebs above it, a single bike (Kevin's) chained to a metal bar bolted to the wall. A woman opened the door almost immediately — maroon tracksuit, unbrushed brown hair and grey eyes set inside dark rings of exhaustion, medication or both.

"Mrs Branston?"

She nodded.

"I work with Kevin. Is he in?"

She frowned as if the question was too hard. She leant forward and looked up the road. "Gone to the shops." Mullen followed her gaze, but could see only a couple of people and they were women with buggies. "He'll be back," she said and withdrew inside, leaving the door open behind her. Mullen took this as an invitation and followed her along a short corridor that led into a long kitchen diner. The near end was the kitchen and every surface was covered with stuff — mostly food (packets, boxes, tins, jars, bottles), but also with books, newspapers, a large grey fairy holding flowers which had been painted a variety of yellow and orange hues, a brass hand-bell and an assortment of kitchen implements and machines.

Mrs Branston went over to the surface to the left of the cooker, pushed some things aside and switched on a kettle.

"I'm Doug," he said.

She turned and looked at him. She had a half-smile on her face, but she emanated sadness. "Gina." She ran her eyes up and down him slowly, as if she was uncertain as to who or what he was. She pursed her lips. "I could paint you," she said and turned back to the kettle.

Mullen moved a couple of steps deeper in. The far end of the room, he now realised, was populated with her painting equipment, though in a more ordered manner: an easel with a blank canvas on it; boxes of what he took to be oil paints laid out on a long flat trestle table which stood along the left-hand wall; brushes and pallet knives; a plate of fruit and a couple of small blue and white vases which he imagined may have been the subject of a still-life; jam jars and bottles of linseed and white spirit. All the paraphernalia was there, but no sign of any painting in progress.

"I could paint you naked," she continued, talking to the wall, "but Kevin is a bit of a prude."

Mullen wasn't sure how to react. He looked around. There was only one painting on the walls; it hung over the trestle table. He went and stood in front of it: a head and shoulders portrait of a younger, thinner Kevin, half-turned towards the artist, yet avoiding her gaze, looking beyond her. It was the sort of pose that photographers favour, endowing their subject with a distant, thoughtful look. But in this case, with the sharp differentiation of dark and light around Kevin's features, Mullen thought he could see something else, a shiftiness, an inability to look his wife squarely in the eye. Or was that his own interpretation, based on his own suspicions with regard to Branston and Diana Downey?

"Sit down."

Mullen turned to see that Gina had crossed the room and was holding out a mug of tea. She picked up a camouflage jacket lying on a tall stool and tossed it aside. "There," she said, pointing. "I want you to look directly at the wall. Below the portrait, not at it."

Mullen did as he was told. She picked up a pad and a couple of pencils from one of the jars, walked back to the main kitchen table and perched on its edge. "You can drink your tea and you can talk if you want, but otherwise I want you to keep still."

Mullen didn't talk. He sat and sipped and concentrated on a dark smudge on the white wall. He could hear her pencil gliding across the paper, long strokes and short strokes, wild flourishes and careful hatching, and occasionally moments of inactivity when the only sound was her muttering not quite soundlessly to herself.

"Now look at me," she said, ripping a sheet from the pad and setting it down beside her. "And put your tea down."

He obeyed. He had never had anyone do this to him before and it felt unsettling, as if he was being examined and found wanting. He watched her face, as her eyes constantly flicked between his face and her pad, absorbed in the present. An ambulance went past outside, but there wasn't even a flicker of distraction. The front door opened. Mullen's eyes moved and took in the puzzled outline of her husband.

"Doug," she snapped, forcing him to face her again. There was exasperation in her voice and she scratched harder and faster with her pencil, fearful that the opportunity was almost gone.

"What's all this then?" There was surprise in Kevin Branston's voice.

"I'm drawing Doug," she said, still wielding her pencil with an air of desperation. "Isn't it obvious?"

"What are you doing here, Doug?" Branston clearly wasn't pleased.

Mullen said nothing. He had reverted to looking at Gina, giving her his fullest attention. He felt irrationally angry that Branston had returned and interrupted her. But the spell had been broken and Gina gave a sigh of disgust. "I haven't finished!"

For a moment Mullen wondered if there was going to be a full-scale argument, but Branston shrugged as if this was normal. "OK. I'm off to the loo." And he turned back along the corridor, taking his newspaper with him, and trudged up the stairs.

Gina returned to her sketch, head bent so low over it that her hair hung down like a curtain. Mullen knew he had to ask his question now or he never would, even if it was a leading one and deceitful too. But the thought had been there ever since the previous evening, and it had put down roots.

"Kevin tells me you suffer from insomnia."

She gave a half laugh from behind the hair. "Something like that."

"Do you find rohypnol helps?" It was a stab in the dark.

For several seconds she made no response, as her pencil continued to skate across the paper. Finally she stopped, raised her head, pushed her hair out of her eyes and regarded Mullen. "He shouldn't have talked about it," she said. "It's none of anyone else's business." It wasn't an admission, but it wasn't a denial either.

"Can I see what you've drawn?" Mullen was more than curious to see what she had made of him, but he also wanted to change the subject.

"No," she said firmly. She tucked her notepad under her arm, picked up the first sketch from the table and then, like her husband, retreated along the corridor and up the stairs. Mullen picked up his mug and drained what was left of the tea. He couldn't shake off the feeling that he had had a great opportunity and blown it.

* * *

"So why exactly are you here?" Kevin Branston said. The irritation in his voice was palpable. Three or four minutes had passed since Gina had disappeared upstairs and he had reappeared. Mullen couldn't help but wonder if and what they had been saying to each other. "This is my home and it is outside of work hours."

"I'm not here about work."

"So what the hell is this visit about?"

"Chris. Chris who drowned in the river."

Branston seemed surprised. He peered at Mullen, his eyes narrowing. "What?"

"I'd like to know why you met Chris in Costa in Queen Street a few weeks ago and gave him a substantial sum of money."

Branston opened his mouth and then shut it. Mullen could see his Adam's apple working overtime. His face had flushed visibly, betraying the anger within. "I think you'd better leave."

"Was he blackmailing you?"

There was no response from Branston.

Mullen pressed. "About your relationship with Diana Downey?"

The blood drained from Branston's face. He wobbled. For a moment, it seemed to Mullen that he was in danger of collapsing on the floor, but he grabbed the work surface with his hand, knocking over a packet of cereal as he did so.

"We aren't having a relationship." His words were barely audible.

"I saw you coming out of the vicarage on Thursday." Mullen paused, allowing the information to sink in. "At two twenty in the afternoon to be precise."

"Look, it's not what you think." Branston went to the sink and poured himself a glass of water. He drank half of it before he continued. "Diana is a friend. A good friend. But that's all. I think she's gay if you must know, though we've never discussed it. She's been very supportive. About Gina that is." He paused, as if wondering how much to say. "Gina has mental health issues. I find it a bit difficult sometimes, coping with it. I met Diana at the Meeting Place first. She came along because she was very interested in what we were doing there. I really appreciated that. And I soon found out that she was a good listener too. So she agreed that I could come and talk to her at the vicarage, well away from work and home. I guess you'd call it informal counselling."

"If it was merely counselling, why did you give Chris money?"

"I'm coming to that." He licked his lips and drank some more water. "Chris was a bastard. He noticed we got on well and he discovered that I was visiting Diana. He joked about how it would be easy for someone to get the wrong idea about it. At least I thought it was a joke. But the next thing was he was telling me how hard up he was and that what he really wanted to do was go and live in Spain. He knew someone there, he said, who would help him get work. But he needed money to get himself there. It was all a load of rubbish, of course. But I was naïve enough to think that if I gave him £500, then at least he would clear off and we'd be shot of him."

"We?" Mullen couldn't help himself from jumping on the word. "So Diana knew about this?"

"No." Branston fell silent for a long moment. Eventually he continued. "What I mean is that Diana knew about Chris's insinuations that we were having a sexual relationship. But I never told her about the £500 I gave him. You have to believe that. It was my own stupid idea. For three days I thought it had worked a treat. Chris disappeared from view. I was really pleased with myself. But then he turned up again at the Meeting Place, a smirk on his face. 'Change of plan,' he told me."

"And did you have a change of plan too?"

He frowned. "What do you mean?"

"Did you decide to kill him?"

"What on earth are you talking about? He fell into the river because he was drunk as a skunk."

Mullen shook his head. "I believe that someone helped him to fall into the river."

"How can you possibly know that?"

Mullen shrugged. "Call it an educated guess."

Branston glared at him. Mullen noticed that his hands had clenched into fists, but it didn't bother him. He was confident that if it came to a fight, he would be more than a match for the guy.

Eventually Branston responded. "You think I did it?"

"As far as I can see, you've certainly got a motive." In truth the longer the conversation had gone on, the less certain Mullen felt about his theory, but it was the only one he had.

"I think you had better leave," Branston said. "Now!"

"As you wish."

* * *

Paul Atkinson very nearly didn't answer the door bell. He had had enough of people calling in to offer their condolences and ask nosey questions. God knew he and Janice hadn't had the best of relationships. A lot of that was his fault. But it was partly hers too. It was hard to live with someone who was always checking up on you. Janice had always wanted to know who he had been meeting for lunch (especially if they were female), what they had been discussing, what the woman was wearing and how old she was. Her enquiries were about as subtle as a sledge hammer. In the end, it had pushed him into having the affairs she was so suspicious about. Not with anyone at St Mark's. That would have been far too risky. Usually it happened on his business trips to the States, where the other party accepted it for what it was — a brief sexual encounter where neither makes any emotional demands on the other. There had been one-night stands in Prague and Berlin too. But he had kept things safely at a distance until Becca. He hadn't been looking for an affair or expecting one. It had just happened and it had been great until Janice found out.

The doorbell rang again, this time more insistently. Whoever it was, they were determined. It was almost certainly someone from the church. He must have had nine or ten people call in over the past two days, each bearing a card of sympathy and each hoping he would let them in for a cup of tea and a chance to 'chat.' He had done just that with some of them — Derek Stanley and Margaret Wilby, Rose, Diana Downey — and they had talked in solemn tones about what a lovely person Janice had been and how unbelievable it was that she could have been taken from them like that. Of course there were things they didn't say, but he could sense they were thinking them. How he hadn't been a very good husband. That if he had been a better one, then somehow poor Janice wouldn't have been run down in the middle of the Iffley Road. And what on earth had she been doing in the Iffley Road at that time of night anyway? Only Margaret Wilby had been honest enough to ask him that particular question and in her usual forthright manner. He hadn't answered her, of course.

Diana Downey had at least offered him practical support, offering to deal with the undertaker and discussing the funeral arrangements. With her help he had already decided on a private cremation followed an hour later by a service back at St Mark's. She had prayed with him too, which he had found comforting and surreal. The whole situation was surreal, of course, and he still hadn't got his head round it. Not to mention the number of phone calls he had had to make to relatives and friends. So the last thing he wanted was to have to be polite to another well-wisher. But that didn't stop the bell ringing yet again, long and loud. He swore and made his way along the hall, bracing himself for whoever it might be. At the door stood probably the last person he expected (or wanted) to see. It was Eddie Loach.

Loach held up both hands in front of his shoulders in mock surrender. "I'm really sorry!" he said. Quite what he was sorry about he didn't make clear. Was it about Janice? Was it about calling at his house in the evening? Or was it because he was such a plonker?

"I'm really tired," Atkinson said.

"It's not about work." Loach lowered his hands. "And it's not about Janice, though obviously we are all in shock in the office."

Atkinson stepped back a couple of paces, gesturing Loach to come in. Loach had never been to his house before. Atkinson was surprised that he even knew where they lived. Probably Human Resources had told him. Or else Doreen. It was more likely Doreen in fact, making sure she kept in his good books because Eddie the Beagle was an ambitious bastard. So why on earth was he here now?

"It's about Doreen."

"Doreen?" The frayed rope which was holding Atkinson's temper and sanity in check pulled a few more loose strands. "I thought you said it's not about work." His voice was savage. "If you can't deal with her, it's your problem."

Loach's sunburnt face wasn't wearing its habitual smile.

"She's dead, Paul."

The words didn't register. Atkinson saw Loach's mouth move and heard the sounds it made. But none of this made an impression on his brain.

"It was a fire," Loach continued. "The flat in which she lived with her mother caught fire. They were both pronounced dead on arrival at the hospital."

"Oh God!" Atkinson's left leg quivered. For a moment he thought he was going to fall down.

Loach moved forward and grabbed him by the arm. "Steady!"

Atkinson began to hyperventilate. Loach guided him to one of the dining chairs and sat him down.

"It's been on the local news." Loach spoke slowly, as if to someone with learning difficulties. "I understand they will be releasing the names shortly. But we didn't want you to find out via a news bulletin or from the Oxford Mail."

"No." He shook his head, but once he had started he found he couldn't stop it shaking. In fact his whole body was shaking. He felt a wave of nausea rising from his stomach and then he was sick across the surface of the table.

Chapter 9

Dorkin was checking out his boat when the phone call came. The boat was, in his eyes, a thing of intricate beauty and breathless speed. It measured 1470 millimetres in length and 284 millimetres in width and it was the closest he was ever going to get to owning — or handling — a mega-yacht. Not that he cared; it was his secret vice. Sailing his immaculate radio-controlled model on a Sunday morning on the artificial lake in Hinksey Park and chatting with the other enthusiasts (all male) kept him sane at the end of a long week. In any case it wasn't truly a vice, even though he liked to think that his craft must provoke feelings of intense covetousness amongst the rest of his fellow aficionados. Nor indeed was it in any proper sense secret because there were plenty of people who could see him indulging his passion as they wandered past on their way to church or the Sunday market, accompanied by children or grandchildren or dogs. It was secret in so far as he had never talked about it at work, for fear that his colleagues might laugh; that the women might think it rather sweet or the men that 'old Dork has gone a bit soft.' Dorkin glanced at the mobile to see who the call was from. Whoever it was he would ignore it.

He swore and pressed answer. "Yes?"

Fargo had never rung him on a Sunday before. They didn't socialise except for a drink or three after work, but that was different, a sort of continuation of work. Ringing him during his time off meant something serious had happened. Or if it hadn't, Dorkin's tongue was primed to tear several strips off Fargo.

"Sorry, sir." It was a sensible start.

"What?" Dorkin spoke sharply. He could sense his day was about to take a very undesirable turn.

"There's something you need to know, sir."

"Is there?"

"There was a fire in Cornwallis Road on Friday night."

"I know."

"Two victims. A Doreen Rankin and her mother."

"And?"

"Doreen Rankin is Paul Atkinson's PA."

Dorkin allowed the information to sink in. Then he said: "Is the fire suspicious?"

Fargo cleared his throat. "No-one is committing themselves at the moment."

"So why ring me on a Sunday morning, Fargo?"

"They found something." Fargo paused. "Something I believe is relevant to our current investigations."

Dorkin growled a warning across the radio waves. "Tell me what they found, Fargo — in nice simple words. Then I'll tell you if it's relevant or not. OK?"

* * *

Walking into St Mark's on the second Sunday in a row was a very different experience for Mullen. The first time he had been expected — indeed invited — by Rose Wilby and he had been an item of interest and curiosity to the whole congregation. He had felt surprisingly nervous about walking into church, but he had also felt welcome. This time, however, it was like walking into a foreign and hostile land. The atmosphere in the church was different.

There was less chattering as people settled down, or at least the chattering was far more subdued. People were talking with lowered voices and faces, conscious of the presence up near the front of the lone figure of Paul Atkinson, who was sitting ram-rod straight and with empty seats either side of him.

A woman with grey curly hair and elegant mid-green top and skirt thrust a service sheet into Mullen's hand and welcomed him. He stepped past her, conscious that there were people behind him, and looked around in the hope of encountering a familiar face.

"Mr Mullen!" The voice came from behind him and he turned. "How nice to see you again. I thought you might have been scared off by us all." Margaret Wilby smiled, but there was no warmth in it, no sense of welcome.

"Perhaps I might sit with you?" Mullen responded, taking her at face value. She was probably the person he least wanted to sit next to. He imagined that she felt the same.

Derek Stanley, standing at her shoulder, stepped forward. "Of course, Doug. Very nice to see you." He spoke in short, halting sentences. "It's going to be rather difficult today, I fear. A time to support each other. Poor Paul." He stumbled to a verbal halt.

"Poor Janice too," Mullen said quickly. It was Janice he felt sorry for. Not the man who had cheated on her. Not the man who might have killed her.

"In a sense, yes." Stanley pulled at his moustache. "But we believe she is now in a better place — and at peace with herself."

Mullen followed them to their pew and sat down. Stanley sat in the middle, probably a deliberate move, Mullen reckoned, to keep him separate from Margaret. Stanley, he had decided, was the peace-maker, albeit a slightly odd one with a singular taste in clothes: today it was an orange polo shirt, rust coloured shorts and leather sandals of the style once favoured by Roman legionaries.

Reverend Diana Downey was as subdued as the rest of them. Her sermon seemed flat and uninspired compared to the previous week — not that Mullen had a whole lot of experience in judging sermons. She spoke of the shock of Janice's death, but said nothing that Mullen didn't already know. There was no date fixed for the funeral yet, she announced. "But do keep Paul and Janice's mother in your prayers."

As the Reverend Downey made her way down the centre of the nave and so signalled the end of the service, Stanley touched Mullen on the arm.

He flinched, caught off guard.

Stanley didn't appear to notice. "Stay for coffee. It's proper coffee, not instant."

"Thank you, I will."

"If you need me to introduce you to people, I will. I guess we must seem rather overwhelming when you're new."

Stanley was right. Mullen did find it challenging. There was part of him that wanted to walk straight out of the church and then keep walking until he was far enough away to open his mouth and scream.

"Don't worry. I'm sure I'll be OK," he lied.

He glanced around. He wanted to ask Margaret Wilby where her daughter was. Their last meeting hadn't finished well and he regretted that. But Margaret Wilby had exited from the pew via the side aisle and was walking up to a man and woman who were settling down onto two chairs in a corner. A shaft of coloured sunshine angled down through the window above, directly onto a third, empty chair. It was on this that Margaret Wilby sat down.

"She has gone for prayer ministry," Stanley said, whispering into Mullen's ear. "Under the watchful eye of St Mark. Anyway let's get some coffee. Come on."

Mullen followed him, down the nave and then left towards the huddle of people queuing for a drink. Never mind St Mark, it felt like Derek Stanley was keeping a watchful eye on him.

"So, would you say you have any sort of Christian faith?" Stanley said as they stood waiting their turn.

"No." In other circumstances — such as with a few glasses of beer inside him — he might have replied in greater detail and told Stanley how he had had some sort of belief in God until his best friend Ben had blown his own brains out one evening in the barracks. But Mullen was currently very sober. More significantly he had just spotted across the other side of the church someone he had never expected to see. It was Charles Speight. There was no doubt about it. He and a woman (his wife, Mullen assumed) were talking to Paul Atkinson.

"None at all?" Stanley said. "So why are you here today?"

"I'm searching for the truth."

"Aren't we all?"

Mullen wished that Stanley would leave him be. He doubted that they were seeking the same truth and in any case he was far more interested in Speight. He gestured in his direction.

"That's Dr Speight with Paul Atkinson isn't it?" He thought he might as well pick Stanley's brains. It would be more useful than being quizzed about his own lack of faith.

"Yes. And his wife Rachel."

"I don't recall seeing them last Sunday."

"Not exactly regular attendees." Stanley's voice hissed with disapproval. "It's amazing how a couple of deaths in the congregation can suck the back-sliders back into the fold."

Mullen opened his mouth to ask more, but he felt a hand on his upper arm.

"Hello, Doug. Just the man I was hoping to see." Rose Wilby was wearing a green short-sleeved top and trousers of a darker green, and her curly hair was more out of control than usual. "Excuse us, Derek." She led Mullen away until they were in the south aisle, enjoying some sort of privacy. Mullen had a moment of déjà vu — a week before he had been hiding behind this very column with Janice.

Mullen assumed Rose had something important to say to him, but for several seconds she stood in front of him in silence. She was breathing fast and chewing on her bottom lip.

Mullen wasn't sure if he owed her an apology or vice versa. Their last meeting really hadn't ended well. He knew that. But he didn't think it had been his fault. Quite the opposite. Rose had obviously been put out by the fact that Becca had been there. A case of good old-fashioned green-eyed jealousy.

"Chris and I were not lovers," she said suddenly. She continued to chew furiously at her lip. "I want to make that absolutely clear to you."

"OK."

"We were friends. Very good friends considering the few weeks we had known each other. But it was nothing more than that."

"It wouldn't matter to me if it was. That would be between the two of you. The only reason I asked was because I was trying to find out more about Chris's death."

"Which I told you to stop doing." Her voice was sharp. "I hired you with Janice's encouragement and now I have released you from your obligations." She moved closer to him, but not for intimacy. "Don't you see? The more you hang around church and the more you ask questions, the more people will look at me and wonder what went on between Chris and me. I'm the youth worker here, don't you understand? My contract is due for renewal this autumn. So it would be best for me if you were to disappear from the scene. Then everyone here would soon forget about Chris and stop speculating about our relationship and I would be able to get on with my life."

"I see." Mullen didn't like it, but he really did start to see. "So you want me to stay away from St Mark's."

"I certainly do."

"I'll try to."

"Thank you." She had stopped chewing at her lip. She looked up at him from under her hair. There was half a smile on her lips. "Sorry if I interrupted your conversation with Derek."

"I think you rescued me, actually."

"Derek can be a bit intense. Devoted to Mummy, of course. I fear she rather exploits that and gets him running errands for her all over the place." Mullen didn't want to talk about Stanley so he changed the subject. "I've started The Lion, the Witch and the Wardrobe, you know."

"Oh!" She was clearly surprised.

Mullen hated to be patronised. Did Rose think he was incapable of reading? Did she think he was stupid?

"Lucy has just gone to Mr Tumnus's house for the second time and has found it ransacked," he said, to prove his point.

"It's a horrid moment." She frowned. Her thoughts were elsewhere. "How is Becca?"

"She was fine when I last saw her. Which was the same day I last saw you." And gossiped about the Reverend Downey he could have added. He looked towards the church door and saw her standing talking to someone he didn't recognise, a woman with red hair who was laughing.

"Sorry. It's none of my business whether you are seeing each other."

"And this may be none of my business, but I am going to ask you anyway. Is the Reverend Downey a lesbian?"

Rose flushed an angry red. "You're dead right. It is none of your business." She turned and moved away a couple of steps, before glancing back at him. She was chewing her lip again. "You can keep the book when you've finished it."

Mullen watched her go, marching purposefully down the aisle, but if she had hoped to escape from the church she was to be disappointed; a huddle of girls intercepted her. Mullen sighed. As an exercise in burying the hatchet, it had been a disaster. He cut through the pews to the nave. He still hadn't had a coffee. He glanced around, looking to see where the Speights had got to, but he couldn't see either of them. Paul Atkinson had moved to the exit where he had ousted the red-haired woman and was talking to Downey. He had taken her right hand with both of his and seemed to be clinging on to it for dear life.

Mullen got his coffee and looked around. It would have been interesting to encounter Speight again. He rather doubted the man would admit to knowing him, but even so it would have been amusing to see how he reacted. However Speight was not in sight. He scanned further, looking for someone he could talk to. Margaret Wilby was advancing determinedly down the nave. She was heading, he suddenly realised, directly towards him.

She gave him a curt nod of greeting. "I couldn't help noticing that you were talking to my daughter."

Mullen nodded. Couldn't help noticing?

"Is everything all right?" she continued, oblivious to his irritation.

"I think Rose and I have a tendency to rub each other up the wrong way."

"Ah!" She pursed her lips as she assessed her next question. "I understood your services had been dispensed with." It was more of a statement, though the underlying question was presumably along the lines of: "So what on earth are you doing in St Mark's today?"

"I rather enjoyed the service last week. I thought I would try it again."

Margaret Wilby made a noise that indicated she didn't believe him for a second. She inclined her head. "Goodbye, Mr Mullen."

Mullen sipped at his coffee. He tried not to care but he was beginning to feel distinctly unwelcome. So when a teenage girl came up and asked him with immaculate politeness if he would be willing to sponsor her on a fun run, he agreed without asking what the cause was and pulled a ten-pound note out of his pocket.

"I'm not doing the run until two weeks' time," she said.

"It doesn't matter," he replied and wrote his details down on her sheet. "I trust you."

"You're the private detective, aren't you?"

"Yes."

"Have you found out what happened to Chris?"

Mullen completed his signature and straightened up. It was hard to know how to respond to such directness. He might not believe in God, but he did believe in being honest. "He drowned in the river down towards Sandford."

"I know that." There was disappointment in her voice. She was clearly expecting a lot more detail. "People say he got drunk and fell in."

Mullen nodded, but didn't comment.

"I think that's rubbish. He didn't drink. He told us."

Mullen felt a flickering of interest.

"Who is 'us'?"

"Our youth group. We meet on Sunday evenings. Diana brought him along the other week to talk to us. She thought it would be good for us to hear his story from his own lips. There are so many down-and-outs on the streets in Oxford and we all tend to ignore them."

Alice — that was the name on her sponsor sheet — spoke with frightening clarity and certainty. "I mean, what should I do if I see them begging in the Cornmarket? Should I give them money? Should I go and buy them a sandwich? Should I just walk on by like most people do? I could pray for them of course, but is that enough?"

Mullen was impressed. He wished he had all the answers. He wished that at her age he had had all the questions too. "Personally, I wouldn't give them money. Maybe buy them a sandwich?"

"I prefer to support the charities which help them," she said decisively. "Diana agrees. Chris agreed too."

Mullen studied Alice. How old was she? Fourteen maybe, going on twenty-four. He changed tack. "So how did Chris come to be sleeping rough in Oxford? Did he tell you his story?"

"He did and he didn't. He said there were a lot of things in his past that he wasn't proud of and preferred not to talk about. What he did say was that he didn't have a very happy childhood and that he was sent away to boarding school and hated it."

"He didn't say what school?"

"No."

"Did he talk about his family?"

"Not really. His parents were killed in a car crash, but that was all he said about them."

"Did he say where he came from? Or if he used to do a job?"

Alice frowned. For the first time, she seemed uncertain. "He was rather evasive about the details."

"Or when and why he came to Oxford?"

"He said he came here because he thought Oxford in the summer would be a rather fine place to be." Alice smiled, remembering. "Those were his exact words. Then he winked."

"Winked? At you?"

"At our youth worker, Rose!" She rolled her eyes. "I think he fancied Rose. And she liked him."

"Lots of people seem to have liked him." Mullen left the statement hanging in the air, hoping Alice might say something else, preferably something indiscreet which would clarify the confusion he felt when he tried to imagine Chris as a person. Chris the elusive, as hard to pin down as a dragonfly.

Alice shrugged. "Thanks for the sponsorship!" And she turned away.

The church was emptying. Mullen watched Alice approach an old lady dressed in purple, but his brain barely registered this because it was too busy sifting the details of their conversation. Chris was rather evasive about detail. That was what the girl had said. If that was the case — and everything he had learnt so far pointed to that being so — the question was: why? What had Chris got to hide?

Mullen downed the last of his coffee and returned the cup to the hatch. He moved towards the exit. The Reverend Downey was talking to yet another member of her congregation. Mullen was relieved. He had had enough. He just wanted to slip unobtrusively out of church and escape back home.

"Doug!" It seemed that the Reverend didn't let members of her congregation sidle past her without a firm handshake and exchange of greetings. "How nice to see you here again! We must be doing something right!" She laughed and took his hand, leaning closer as she did so. "I gather you've been talking to Kevin," she said in a low whisper. "I trust you haven't been jumping to any wild conclusions?" Her fingers tightened their grip. "You should read the epistle of James. It cautions us all about the dangers of idle gossip." Her fingernails dug into the back of his hand. Then she released her hold and smiled. "See you next Sunday, I hope."

* * *

Mullen exited the church with a sigh, but there was little relief outside. The relative cool of the church was exchanged for the heat of another scorching day. There was no protection from the blazing light of the sun either and as he lifted his right hand against it he glimpsed two figures standing dark and still a couple of metres in front of him.

"Well, well, well, if it isn't Mr Mullen."

He recognised the sarcastic voice of Dorkin immediately, just as he recognised the bulky outline of DS Fargo. He felt a jolt of anxiety. He didn't need Sherlock Holmesian powers to deduce that something was very wrong.

"A little bird told us you'd be at church," Dorkin continued. "Didn't really believe it, but what do you know?" Dorkin was enjoying the moment.

A thought flashed across Mullen's brain: who was the little bird? But then it was gone and Dorkin was saying something else. "I'd like a little chat with you, Mullen, if you don't mind."

"It's Sunday," Mullen said, stating the obvious.

"Normally it's my day off too," came the reply. Dorkin had dropped the sarcasm. "But I have here a search warrant," he said. "For The Cedars, Foxcombe Road, Boars Hill." He thrust a piece of paper at Mullen. "Would you like to read it?"

Mullen was suddenly conscious that there were several members of the St Mark's congregation standing around, watching with fascination. Rose Wilby and Derek Stanley were both standing on the far side of the road. They must have left shortly before he had and had turned to watch the drama unfold. Mullen tried to ignore them. He glanced at the search warrant in his hand. He made no attempt to read it in detail. He hadn't ever seen one before, but it could hardly be a fake. Dorkin wouldn't be stupid enough to do that, especially with so many curious bystanders as witnesses. He handed it back to him. "So what now?"

'What now?' involved Mullen handing over his house keys to Dorkin, who passed them over to a pair of uniformed officers standing in the shade of one of the poplar trees which stood in ranks along the front of the church.

'What now?' involved Mullen himself being driven to the police station and then having to wait for nearly two hours before a solicitor could be found.

'What now?' involved Mullen in doing a lot of thinking.

* * *

Mullen's solicitor introduced herself as Althea Potter. She was brisk and a little off-hand. She was dressed in white slacks and pale pink blouse. Her blonde bob of hair was still wet and she smelt of chlorine. She looked like a woman who had just had her weekend rudely interrupted.

She asked Mullen a series of questions, made a note of his answers on her notepad and then went to the door. There was a uniformed constable outside. "Tell Inspector Dorkin we are ready," she said. "And would you mind getting us both a cup of tea. I would also point out that my client hasn't had lunch either."

Twenty minutes passed before Dorkin appeared with Fargo. Mullen tried not to give way to his feelings of irritation. No doubt this delaying was a deliberate tactic by Dorkin, but if so the constable who brought in not just cups of tea but also sandwiches was not party to it. Mullen was starting to feel human again.

Fargo did the preliminaries. Then he fell silent and waited for Dorkin who again embarked on a game of silence as he leafed through the folder of papers lying on the table in front of him.

"What the heck is this all about?" Mullen said. Althea Potter touched his arm with her hand, but he had no intention of lying there and being trampled.

Dorkin looked across at him, a jackal-smile on his face. "I've got something to show you," he said.

Fargo conjured up with a flourish a thin large-format book out of the pile of paperwork in front of him and placed it in front of Mullen. Mullen didn't have to fake surprise. He had never seen the book in his life, as far as he was aware.

"Art isn't my thing," he said.

"What about photography?"

Fargo did his conjuror act again and placed three photographs on the table. "Do you recognise these?"

Mullen nodded. "Of course. I took them. When I was working for Janice Atkinson."

"And who are the people in them?"

"Paul Atkinson and Becca Baines."

"Good. That was easy wasn't it? So you took these photos and gave them to Janice?"

"Yes."

"Did you give her printed copies like these or did you give her digital copies?"

Mullen picked up each photo in turn, examining the back.

"These are some of the prints I gave her. There's a number in pencil on the back. That was me. I kept the digital files myself."

"A couple of nights ago, a woman died in a house fire. These photographs were found inside this book under her body."

For the first time, Mullen felt a surge of panic. "Who was she?"

Dorkin didn't reply.

The room was surprisingly cool, but Mullen could feel the sweat on his forehead. "Jesus, it wasn't Becca, was it?" Dorkin was eyeing him steadily.

There was a hiss of anger from Mullen's right. "Stop messing about, Inspector." Althea Potter, hitherto silent, stabbed her pen onto her notepad. "My client has come here willingly. He has agreed to cooperate with your investigations. But if you persist, I will advise him to withdraw that cooperation."

Dorkin's face twitched. "The dead woman was a Doreen Rankin. She worked for Paul Atkinson."

Mullen tried to think. So did that mean Janice had shown her husband the photographs? If so, how come Doreen had got them? Was she another lover?

He looked up. Dorkin was shifting in his seat and asking him another question.

"Why did you think that the dead woman might be Becca Baines?"

Mullen tried to think. "I don't know. The photo I suppose. You said it was a woman . . ." He tailed off. When the hell had he last seen Becca? His brain was porridge.

"Are you and Becca lovers?"

"There's no need to answer that," Althea Potter intervened.

Mullen shrugged. "I'll answer it if the Inspector will answer one of my questions. Was the fire an accident or was it arson?"

Dorkin returned his stare. Then he answered. "The circumstances which gave rise to the fire are uncertain."

Mullen smiled back. "And the relationship between myself and Becca Baines is also uncertain."

"Do you have any other questions for my client?" Althea Potter was clearly impatient to rescue what was left of her Sunday.

Dorkin turned to Fargo and nodded. Fargo removed the book and photographs from the table and delved again into his pile of paperwork. This time he produced a see-through evidence bag and placed it in front of Mullen.

"Do you recognise this?"

Mullen picked it up, studied the pills inside the bag and then replaced it on the table. "No."

"For the record, we found them inside the Cedars, Foxcombe Road, Boars Hill."

"They must be the professor's."

"We'll check that out."

"What is in the bag?" Althea Potter's manner betrayed the fact that she was getting increasingly irritated by every sentence that passed Dorkin's lips.

"Rohypnol."

"And what is the relevance of finding rohypnol in my client's place of residence?"

Dorkin shrugged. "It may not be relevant. I just wanted to check it out."

"Check it out?" Althea Potter spat the words back at Dorkin one at a time as if they were some unexpectedly sour berries. She had had enough. She began to gather up her papers. "I think my client has answered quite enough questions for now. Unless, of course, you are going to charge him with a crime?"

Mullen should have kept his mouth shut. He knew that even as he opened it. But sometimes common sense makes no sense. "Janice Atkinson had rohypnol in her bloodstream when she died," he announced.

Dorkin, Fargo and Potter all stared at him.

"As did Chris, who was found floating face down in the river."

They were all still staring. In silence.

"And just for the record," Mullen concluded, "I know because the pathologist Charles Speight told me."

* * *

For a few marvellous seconds, Mullen had been more pleased with himself than he could possibly have imagined. Dorkin's face, contorted in disbelief, was a joy to behold. But after the high comes the low. And by the time Althea Potter had given him several pieces of her mind and then departed in a swirl of anger, Mullen was realising that what he had said hadn't been very clever at all. He was also realising that for the second time he was stuck in the Cowley police station a long way from his car, which he had left in what was fast becoming his personal parking space in South Oxford. It would take him an hour or so to walk, he reckoned, as he pushed his way out through the exit doors.

"Hi!"

Rose Wilby was standing a few metres away, leaning against the metal railings and holding a cigarette. She dropped it hastily and ground it out with her foot.

"Bad habit. Don't tell my mother."

Mullen stood still. He felt awkward, unsure of his own thoughts and feelings. "Mum's the word," he replied, because he didn't trust himself to say anything more real.

"Would you like a lift?"

He nodded.

She advanced towards him. "Good." Then, to his surprise, she put her arms round him and held him for several seconds. "Sorry," she said finally, releasing him.

She drove him back to South Oxford in silence. Only when she had pulled up opposite his Peugeot in Lincoln Road did she speak again.

"Do you want to talk about it?"

He wondered what she meant by 'it.' Becca? Being questioned by the police? "Not here," he said.

"Shall we go to your house?"

"The police are searching it."

"Ah." She nodded. She didn't sound surprised that the police were combing his house. Mullen tried to read her face for signs, but he drew a blank.

"My flat, then," she said finally. "Follow me. I can give you a visitor's permit to park in the street."

* * *

Rose's flat was a modern one-bedroom spacious affair with a balcony overlooking the river. Expensive for a youth worker, Mullen imagined. In fact way above her salary scale. Not that he had any informed knowledge of what church youth workers were paid, but he doubted it covered the cost of renting a flat in this part of Oxford, let alone buying one. You are what you do. Someone had said that to him once. He wasn't sure who, but it had stayed with him. Now that he had set himself up as a private investigator, he was realising how true it was. All of a sudden he was looking at everyone he encountered with jaundiced, analytical eyes, searching for things that didn't fit. Even Rose Wilby was coming under his baleful gaze. It was possible that Margaret Wilby had bought the flat for her, even though the mother-daughter relationship wasn't the best he had ever encountered. Or had Rose inherited money from her father? A father hadn't ever been mentioned. Had he died or walked out on them? Mullen caught himself glancing around for family photographs, but there were none in the main living space. If Rose had any, he supposed she must keep them in her bedroom.

Rose had been busying herself at the kitchen end of the living space, getting them each a cold drink.

"Homemade lemonade," she announced. "With lots of ice."

They sat down opposite each other at the dining table, hiding from the sun. Mullen took a sip, nodded appreciatively and started to talk. She was a good listener, alert and attentive, saving any questions until he had finished. Even then, she didn't say anything at first. Instead she stood up and drew the long curtains half-way across the balcony windows, shutting out more of the light. Then she moved back and sat down again.

"Tell me about rohypnol."

"It is prescribed to people with sleeping problems. It's a powerful drug and when combined with alcohol causes people to get extremely unsteady and black out. It is popularly known as a date-rape drug. People use it because afterwards victims often have no clear memory of what happened to them."

"How horrible."

Mullen sipped at his drink. It was horrible. Rose was right. But could she really be so innocent as to not know about the drug at her age?

"And they found some where you live."

"It's not mine."

"You could have found it. And you could have used it."

"But I didn't."

"That's what the police will think, isn't it?" Rose said all this in a matter-of-fact way. "That you might have found it and given it to Chris and Janice before you killed them."

"But I didn't." Mullen suddenly felt defensive. He had thought Rose was on his side, but here she was making a case against him. "Don't you believe me?"

"Of course." She stretched out her hand and for a second allowed it to rest on his. "But it doesn't look good, Doug."

This time Mullen took another, slower pull at his lemonade.

"Do you have alibis that someone else can confirm?"

Mullen shook his head. It was something he had thought about too.

"It was you who found Chris, wasn't it? That won't look good either. And you took those photographs for Janice and then she was killed."

"Hell, I know that." He didn't mean to snap, but it was hard not to. "Don't you think I feel guilty about her? If I hadn't gone snooping for her, she wouldn't have come looking for me in the Iffley Road and she would still be alive."

"Stop feeling sorry for yourself, Doug." Rose sounded like her mother. "We need to make a plan and we need to get on with it before the police come knocking on your door again."

* * *

"You're the detective. Don't you have a prime suspect?" Rose had just made them a second glass of lemonade with plenty of ice. It was ridiculously hot in the flat, even with the balcony doors pulled wide open. "I mean, the prime suspects for Janice must be her husband or her husband's lover. Paul or Becca. Or both, of course."

"But why would they kill Chris?" Mullen was talking as much to himself as to Rose.

"How can you be sure Chris was murdered?"

"The rohypnol."

"Maybe someone just gave it to him. Maybe he thought it was some other drug. He took it, had a drink and then fell into the river. That's the simple answer isn't it?"

"Why did you and Janice hire me in the first place?"

Rose shrugged. "Because we liked him."

"That's it?"

"We felt we owed him."

"Owed him what?"

"Not to be forgotten. Not to be ignored just because he was a drifter, a man with no place in society and no fixed abode."

"What about everyone else at St Mark's?"

"A few people agreed. Mostly women. However, I suspect that the majority of people in the church thought we should just leave it to the police."

"And was there anyone who was actively hostile to your plans? Anyone who tried to dissuade you?"

Rose frowned. Not for the first time Mullen realised he found her rather attractive. She wasn't a conventional beauty, but then he had never been drawn to conventional beauties.

"The vicar of course. Diana didn't like Chris. She hid it well. She was perfectly nice to him, but . . ." Rose paused, allowing Mullen to interrupt.

"But she was worried about the effect he was having on her congregation? On people like Janice and yourself?"

"I guess so."

"Anyone else apart from Diana?"

"My mother." Rose laughed at the thought. "She definitely didn't like the way Chris flirted with me."

"Why not?"

"Being nice to him in church was one thing. But any sort of relationship would have been quite another thing in my mother's book."

"And did you respond to any of his flirtations?"

There was a slight pause before she answered his question. "No."

Mullen considered this for a few seconds before moving on. "So when you came and told me you wanted me to stop the investigation, who put you up to it?"

"Diana and my mother essentially. But Janice had got cold feet too. That was what we talked about the last time I spoke to her. She and Rachel Speight waited behind at the end of the youth group. They said they wanted to offer me some 'good Christian advice.'"

"That was it? Did none of the men offer you 'good Christian advice?'"

Rose frowned again, as if that was something she had not considered before. "There was Derek Stanley of course. Wherever my mother goes, he follows in her footsteps. But in my experience, men are less keen to hand out free advice."

"Tell me about Derek."

"What is there to know? He was here at St Mark's when my mother and I came ten years ago."

"Does he have any family?"

"Not that I'm aware of."

"He had a sister, didn't he? Lived in Hungerford. She committed suicide."

Rose opened her eyes wide. "Gosh. You are well informed."

"She was in Hungerford the day Michael Ryan ran amok and killed fourteen people. According to Derek, she was lucky not to be killed herself. Exactly one year later she hanged herself."

She stood up and walked over to the balcony windows, staring out across the river. Mullen studied her profile and was struck by her nose, long and slightly upturned at the end, suggesting an arrogance that was at odds with what he knew of her character. She turned towards him. "How on earth did you get Derek to tell you that?"

"I guess it was the fact that when Chris first came to St Mark's, he was dressed in camouflage fatigues. I asked him about Chris when I met him in church and that was the memory it sparked in him. Michael Ryan and Chris both dressed in army gear."

Rose returned to the table and sat down. "So what are you going to do now? I'd like to help if I can."

Mullen scratched hard at his head. He wasn't sure why, but his scalp had become very itchy. Residue from the bandaging he supposed.

"There's one thing you can do for me," he said. "You can ring Paul Atkinson and tell him you need to see him urgently."

"Paul?" Rose was clearly surprised by Mullen's change of direction. "You don't think that Paul . . . ?"

She tailed off, unable to voice in full what Mullen's request might imply.

"I don't at the moment know of any connections between Paul and Chris, but if anyone were to draw up a list of suspects for the death of Janice, then Paul would be at or near the top."

"As would Becca, surely?"

Mullen said nothing. He knew Rose was right, but it wasn't Becca he was interested in right this moment. He could access Becca himself. In Paul's case, he needed help. "Paul avoided me in church this morning. He doesn't like me. I understand that. But I need to ask him questions. So I want you to arrange a meeting without mentioning that I will be there too."

The meeting proved remarkably easy to arrange. Rose rang Paul Atkinson from her mobile. He picked up almost immediately and when she said how she really needed to talk to him about Chris, he agreed without any further questioning. But as they discussed when and where to meet, Mullen was barely listening. For the suspicious invisible gremlin which sometimes lurked on his shoulder had materialised and started to whisper into his ear. Did you notice, the gremlin said, that the lovely Rose has Paul Atkinson's phone number stored on her phone? What is that all about? The gremlin had plenty more to say. Rose is jealous of Becca Baines and Becca Baines was having an affair with Paul Atkinson — you haven't forgotten that, Doug? But now Becca Baines has been chumming up to you, Doug, even though it was you who put the kibosh on her fun with Paul. And, the gremlin continued, just in case Doug had missed the point, this is not the first time Rose has rung Paul Atkinson mobile to mobile. Put all that in your pipe and smoke it, Doug, the gremlin concluded triumphantly. Afterwards, you can tell me what you make of it.

And Mullen really didn't know what to make of it all. What he did know, however, was that he had to do something if he wanted to get to the bottom of the two deaths. Or should that be three deaths? It was the gremlin again. What about Doreen Rankin? I am not saying that her death is necessarily suspicious, but why, Doug, did the police question you about it? Was it merely because of the photographs they found? Or did they suspect foul play? Mullen's response was that the police didn't quiz him for an alibi; so the likelihood was that the woman's death was just an unfortunate accident. Maybe she fell asleep halfway through a cigarette? Or after lighting a candle? Accidents happen. Why would there be anything intrinsically suspicious about a house fire, unless — the thought hit Mullen like a clapper in a church bell — Doreen Rankin's remains happened to contain traces of rohypnol.

"Is everything OK?" Rose was looking at him with that frown of hers.

"Yes," he said. "You did a good job with Paul." He stood up and drained what was left of his lemonade. "Where are we meeting him?"

"At my mother's."

* * *

Mullen's mobile beeped a second time. It was lying on the table in front of him. His immediate impulse was to pick it up. He hardly ever got text messages. Janice had been the exception. She had sent him a text per day at first, checking on how he was getting on with the job. The frequency of the texts had increased, at first gradually and then exponentially. They had changed in content and tone too, becoming more personal and more desperate. He didn't think he had received any texts from anyone since Janice's death.

He glanced round the room. Paul seemed to be avoiding looking at him, as he had done for much of the visit. If he had noticed the beeps they didn't seem to bother him. Margaret had picked up her tea cup and was watching him as she sipped at it. He was pretty sure that Margaret would disapprove if he checked his mobile in the middle of a meeting. She would consider it bad manners and tell him so very clearly. So he sat back on the sofa and resumed questioning Paul Atkinson.

"Was Janice very friendly with Chris?"

"Does it matter?"

"I'm just asking."

"And I'm asking you — do you seriously think Janice had it in her to kill Chris? And do you also think that she was so filled with remorse that she walked in front of a car to end it all? Because if you do, let me tell you that you are even stupider than you look."

In normal circumstances, Mullen would have taken exception to being called stupid, especially by a waste of space like Paul Atkinson, but these were not normal circumstances.

He rubbed his chin as he worked out his next line of attack and his mobile beeped again, pleading for a response. Mullen pretended not to have heard it.

Margaret Wilby, who had been sipping her tea, put her cup down on her saucer and intervened. "Do feel free to check your messages, Mr Mullen," she said with a glacial smile. Her mouth was small and when she spoke she did so with the minimum of movement, a characteristic which served to emphasise the disapproval her utterances often conveyed. "It may be something important."

Mullen leant forward, unlocked his phone and opened the first message.

"Well?" Margaret Wilby clearly expected him to share his trivial messages with all of them.

"It's Becca," he announced, surprised. "Becca Baines."

It was Rose who reacted first. "Oh?" The single word was laced with layers of meaning: disappointment, irritation and above all jealousy.

"Oh, shit," Mullen said, confirming all of Margaret Wilby's deepest prejudices about him.

"Bad news?" she said.

"I have to go. Sorry."

"What a shame!" Paul Atkinson commented with ill-disguised sarcasm.

* * *

Rose Wilby followed Mullen outside, which was the last thing he wanted. He pretended not to have noticed, but as he set off at a fast walk along the road — it was only 500 yards to where he was parked outside her flat — he could hear her sandals clipping on the pavement as she tried to catch up.

"Doug!" Rose's call was sharp and commanding. For a moment she could have been her mother. But Rose wasn't her mother and Mullen couldn't bring himself to treat her so. He slowed down, half turning, and allowed her to close the gap.

"You remind me of a dog," she said as she came alongside him.

Mullen said nothing. He didn't want to talk.

"Becca whistles and you go scampering off to find her no matter what the circumstances."

"Is that what your mother said?"

"It's what I say, Doug."

Mullen reverted to silence. It seemed safer.

"I thought we were in this together, Doug." Rose's tone had now mutated to plaintive. It was also, as Mullen realised, manipulative. "I don't understand," she said.

They came to a crossing point on their route and waited for a supermarket delivery van to pass in front of them. It gave Mullen time to phrase a reply. He already had a plan half-formulated.

"I think Becca is in trouble." That much was true.

"What sort of trouble?"

"I'm not sure," he said. "That's what I need to go and find out."

"And am I welcome or not?" She was still plaintive.

"Yes." They were in sight of his car and her flat.

"So I can come with you in your car?"

He pointed down at her feet. "You're not going to be much use to me in those. You'll need better footwear."

"OK. I won't be long. Thanks, Doug." She pecked him on the cheek and skittered across the road towards the apartments.

"There's no rush," he called after her, lying.

Mullen pressed in Becca's number. It rang twice before someone answered it. Or rather they didn't answer. All he could hear was heavy breathing. Mullen waited, listening intently. Who the hell was it? Branston? Stanley? Speight even? They were all on Mullen's mental list.

Then he heard a woman's voice. "Is that you Doug?"

"Jesus! Are you alright?"

"Sort of." She didn't sound alright.

"Where are you?"

"Outside your house."

Mullen felt the tension retreat further. "So what's the matter?"

"I need to see you, Doug. I'm scared. Really scared."

"What are you scared of?"

There was a pause before she replied. "Someone has been following me."

"Just wait there. Lock your car doors. I'll be with you in ten minutes."

Mullen glanced across towards the entrance to the flats. There was no sign of Rose. That was good. He got into his car and started the engine. The last thing he needed was her getting in the way and complicating things. If Becca was in danger, there was no time to lose. Besides, one woman who needed protecting was quite enough. He slipped into first gear, released the handbrake and moved off without a backward glance.

* * *

When Mullen swung into the drive of the Cedars, he was expecting to see Becca's red Fiat Punto standing on the gravel. It wasn't there. He stopped ten metres short of the house and switched off. He felt himself tense. Where the heck was she? He opened the door, got out and stood there for several seconds, listening. Not a sound. Nothing significant anyway. There was a mower being gunned across some distant lawn and children giggling and screaming, but there was nothing close at hand. He continued to wait. He could hear vehicles now, advancing along the road from the Oxford direction. He hesitated a moment or two longer before running forward swiftly and stealthily, slightly crouched as if expecting someone to take a pot-shot at him any moment. The sound of gravel crunching under his feet was muffled by the engine noise from the road. He reached the corner of the house and stopped. Looking down as he reviewed his next move, he noticed tell-tale tyre marks on the lawn and the tension inside him eased a notch. He peered round the corner and saw, as he thought he would, Becca's red car pulled up under the large oak some fifteen metres away. He looked for the outline of a figure in the front seat, but there was none. Had she gone into the house? He advanced cautiously across the grass, eyes scanning left and right, until he reached the car and peered in through the side window.

Becca was lying on the back seat, arms clasped round her legs in a foetal position. His first thought was that she was terrified and alive, his second that she was extremely dead. He wrenched the driver's door open and for a few milliseconds hope and fear grappled together on the edge of the abyss. Then Becca Baines screamed.

* * *

Rose had never been stood up before and for several seconds she stood in the parking area outside her block of flats unable to comprehend why Mullen wasn't there. He wasn't the sort of guy to do that sort of thing, surely? That had been her assessment, but clearly she had misjudged him. She walked over to the road, but there was definitely no sign of Mullen or his car; just an empty space where his scruffy green Peugeot had been parked.

Rose wasn't a woman who swore, even in private, but the words came out nevertheless. But swearing changed nothing — it didn't cause Mullen to magically reappear nor did it make her feel any better. She retraced her steps, back to the entrance and then up the two flights of stairs to her apartment. She knew she was on the verge of bursting into tears and she had no desire to do so in public. She had barely slammed the door behind her when her mobile rang. She pulled it out of her bag and studied it. It was her mother. She let it carry on ringing until it kicked into the answering service.

She went to the kitchen, poured herself a glass of water and tried to think. But thinking wasn't very profitable because whichever path her thoughts started out on, they always seemed to end up at the same place with the same bitter thought: Mullen prefers Becca to you and doesn't have the guts to say so.

* * *

Mullen started by giving Becca a cup of tea. She had wept all over him when she got out of the car, clasping him tight, but now as she sat at the kitchen table, she was still and silent, hugging herself and staring vacantly down at the table. Mullen hadn't seen her like this before. He added a couple of sugars to her mug. He didn't know if she was technically in shock, but it seemed to be the right thing to do. Anyway, when she took her first sip she showed no sign of objecting to the sweetness.

Mullen sat down opposite her. "Do you want to tell me about it?"

She sipped at her tea and sniffed.

Mullen tried another approach. "You said on the phone that someone was following you."

She sniffed again and wiped her nose with a tissue extracted from her sleeve. "I wasn't sure at first. I noticed this car following me the other evening. I'd been out to Horspath to visit a friend and it was behind me when I left her house and it was still behind me when I parked my car. To be honest, I didn't think anything of it at the time. In fact I probably wouldn't have noticed him if he hadn't been one of those drivers who tailgate you."

"The driver was a man then?"

"I can't be sure. The headlights were bright. I guess I assumed it was a man because it's usually men who drive like that."

"What about the colour and make of the car?"

"I'm not that much of an expert on cars, and it was getting dark."

"OK," Mullen said, though he felt disappointed and slightly suspicious at her vagueness.

Becca continued. "Then, the next evening, I noticed this person hanging around across the road. It was a guy, wearing army fatigues."

"Would you recognise him if you saw him again?"

She shrugged, sipping her tea.

"I doubt it. He was wearing one of those peaked caps with material hanging down the back and sides against the sun, so really I didn't get much of a view of his face. And it was quite dark of course."

Mullen shivered. Camouflage clothing. He had a sudden flash of memory: Gina Branston tossing a camouflage jacket off the stool just before she began to sketch him. But why would either of the Branstons be following Becca? Did they even know her? Or was it because he and Becca were friends?

Becca tipped her head back and drained her mug of tea. "Haven't you got anything stronger?" she said. "Gin ideally. Or Vodka. Preferably without the added sugar." She raised her eyes. "That was probably the worst cup of tea I have drunk since I was a schoolgirl with plaits."

Mullen got up and made his way towards the larder. He found it hard to imagine Becca with plaits even as a girl. They were so old-fashioned and that wasn't a word he would have applied to her. But it wasn't as if he had known her for long or knew her well. One thing he did know about her was that she was a woman who ploughed her own furrow in life, so maybe she did once wear plaits, if only to be different.

"So what made you think he was watching you? Or indeed that he was watching anyone?" Mullen had located some gin and two small cans of slim-line tonic. It was lucky she wanted gin because that was the only alcohol in the larder. Mullen wondered if the Thompsons had a stash locked away in one of the other rooms. Two generous measures of alcohol later (plus ice and tonic) and he was ready to resume the conversation.

"You think I'm paranoid? Imagining things?" she said.

He put her drink in front of her and settled down opposite her with his.

"No."

"Hell, Doug, if you think I'm being paranoid, say so. I'm not interested in being humoured." She picked up her glass and took a swig followed almost immediately by another. "I thought he was here, in the garden. I heard noise, a bang like someone knocking something over and then I . . ." Becca stopped and plonked her glass on the table with a bang. She stood up. "I'm going to the loo. Why don't you check the garden, see if you can see any signs of the guy?"

Mullen took a swig from his glass as he watched her disappear along the corridor.

Actually he did think she was being a bit paranoid. Or he would have done if he hadn't received that early morning call from a man threatening his friends. And Becca was definitely a friend. He had thought about the man's voice a lot, trying to connect it to someone, but whoever it was he knew exactly what he was doing. The fact was it could have been nearly anyone. Mullen had presumed it was a man, but now he wondered if he could be sure even of that, since the voice had been synthesised. Mullen sipped at his glass and got up. It wouldn't hurt to check the garden. At the very least it would demonstrate to Becca that he was taking her seriously. He walked through to the scullery, unbolted the side door and stepped outside. He took another slug of gin and tonic, plus one for luck and then put his glass down on the teak garden table. The garden was at least an acre in size, with plenty of bushes for someone to be hiding behind. If anyone was out there, and they were armed, then he was going to be in trouble. He started by standing very still and looking and listening. There was nothing that caught his eye or ear. He picked up a spade which was leaning against the wall and headed down the lawn towards the bushes and trees. If anyone was hiding, that had to be the most likely place. If he or she had a gun, he would be in trouble, but otherwise a spade made a very good close-quarter weapon. He pushed his way through the bushes and into the more open space under the big trees. There was no-one.

He took a different route back, along the boundary to his right leading up to the kitchen garden area. Overhead, a red kite whistled and drifted idly on the up currents, looking for prey. Mullen looked up, admiring its grace, and yawned. He resumed his walk and felt his legs wobble underneath him. He shook his head. Maybe drinking gin and tonic in the middle of a scorching day wasn't such a good idea. He smiled as he drew closer to the vegetables. The two tomato plants which he had planted outside the greenhouse were trussing up nicely with fruit. He stopped and knelt down, peering at the promised harvest and then pinching out a few side shoots. It was while he was in the middle of this process that he froze. Beyond the two plants, there were deep footprints in the soft soil where he had only recently planted a second crop of lettuces and radishes. They weren't his and they didn't look like Becca's either. The prints were smaller than his own feet — size eight he reckoned — and they were boots. Not women's boots, to be sure, or wellingtons, but more like working boots. Or army boots. He had seen enough of those in his short military career.

Mullen stood up as casually as he could and looked around, scanning the garden again. But it was as if he was on a roundabout and the world was rotating around him. He felt quite giddy. Not to mention tired. As if he had drunk too much.

But he hadn't drunk too much, just a few gulps of gin. Suddenly he knew exactly what it must be. It was rohypnol. Becca had spiked his drink. It was like a punch in the gut. Becca! He hadn't seen that coming at all. He had trusted her, liked her. And she had betrayed him. But why? His brain came up with no answers. Was she an accomplice to someone? Names drifted into his consciousness — Paul Atkinson, Derek Stanley, Kevin Branston — before popping like soap bubbles in the wind. But then, in an instant, it all became ridiculously obvious. Becca Baines worked at the hospital, didn't she? She was a nurse. No doubt she was used to administering drugs to help people sleep, so getting hold of rohypnol wouldn't be difficult for her. How stupid he had been! Mullen's head was thumping like a big bass drum. He held it between his two hands as he staggered up the path to the kitchen door. Thank God he hadn't drunk all his gin. If he could just get to his mobile, which he had left on the kitchen table, he could ring for help. But who could he trust? Rose? Dorkin?

He pushed the door open and it slammed against the wall. He cursed himself for being a clumsy idiot! There was no sign of Becca, but if blundering around like an elephant on speed didn't bring her back into the kitchen, nothing would. Mullen saw with relief that his mobile was still there on the table. He stumbled across the tiled floor and grabbed at it, but his fingers refused to cooperate with his brain. The handset twisted out of their grip, bounced back down onto the table and then over the far side onto the floor.

It was a long table. Mullen began to edge his way round it. He felt as if he was wading through quick-drying concrete. He got round to the end and saw the mobile lying against the skirting board. Its light was still on. It had survived the fall. Mullen moved his left leg forward, but it encountered something solid and unyielding. He looked down, puzzled by the shape beneath him, and then, like a slow motion video, he was falling down, down, down until his head cracked against the floor. Pain echoed round his skull. Everything went black. Was this what death was like — a mixture of pain and oblivion? He wanted to swear and call out, but he couldn't do either. He lay there for several seconds before he managed to force his eyes open. His mobile was only inches from his head. He strained to reach it, but his body was no longer part of him. Somehow his left hand responded to the urgings of his brain and crept towards the mobile. He felt its familiar shape. His fingers closed round it like a claw and pulled it towards him. But then he heard the sound of footsteps from the front hall, approaching the room, and he knew he was too late.

* * *

In the end, Rose had stopped wallowing in self-pity and come up with a plan. There was only one way to sort this out she had realised and that was to go to the Cedars and confront Mullen — and if he wasn't there she'd wait until he did turn up. And if Becca Baines turned up too, so much the better. She could have it out with both of them. What would she say to Mullen? What might he say to her? The possibilities didn't bear thinking about. So instead she concentrated on getting to Boars Hill without giving way to tears or hysterics.

She was concentrating on herself with such intensity that she very nearly overshot the Cedars. She squealed to a halt in front of the entrance and froze. The driveway was blocked by a police car. She killed her engine and sat there unmoving, as possibilities too horrible to contemplate raced through her head. She shivered, despite the heat of the day. Eventually she bullied herself into getting out of the car. She walked down the drive, past the police car and up the very slight incline towards the house. She was conscious of the gravel crunching under the sensible lace-up shoes that Mullen had insisted would be necessary. There was another car parked up by the house, but it certainly wasn't Mullen's. There were two people standing there talking, a female uniformed officer and a very big man in a suit that was struggling to contain his bulk. Their faces turned in unison. The big man was Detective Sergeant Fargo. He had interviewed her with Dorkin. A man like Fargo, once encountered, is hard to forget (especially when he is named after your favourite Cohen brothers' film).

"Miss Wilby," he said advancing towards her with huge strides. He was holding his right hand up in front of him like a policeman whose secret wish (never fulfilled) had always been to direct the traffic. "You can't come in here."

"What's happened? Is Doug all right?"

"Mr Mullen is not here." The two of them stopped. Fargo was a single pace away from her and she could see the sweat on his face. He looked unhappy with life. "You must leave," he said.

"Is Becca here?" she said. Fargo's eyes opened wider, his interest piqued. "Doug had a text from her," she continued. "She said she was in trouble and needed his help."

"When was this?" She had certainly got his attention.

She shook her head, as if so doing would clear it. At least, she told herself, Doug is alive. "About an hour ago. Or maybe a bit more."

He nodded, as if this made sense or fitted in with what he knew.

"So you were with him when he got the message?"

"Yes. We were in South Oxford. We had just been visiting my mother and . . ."

"Did you see the text?" Fargo spoke with surprising gentleness.

"No. He just told me about it as we were walking to his car."

"Did he say anything else?"

Rose faltered. Fargo was looking at her with a slightly furrowed forehead as if he could sense the dilemma inside her. "I wanted to help him," she said. "He told me I wouldn't be any use to him in my sandals, so I went into my flat to change and when I went outside again he had gone."

Fargo nodded. "I see. That's very helpful."

Rose didn't like the idea that she had been helpful, not if, as she suspected, being 'helpful' meant she had confirmed the police's suspicions of Mullen. "So why are you here?" she said with sudden aggression, "if neither Doug nor Becca is here?"

There was a guttural noise from behind Fargo. Rose peered round his bulk. It was Dorkin. He was standing on the top step of the doorway. She had no idea how long he had been there or how much of the conversation he had heard. All she knew was that she preferred Fargo.

"Ms Baines has been taken to hospital," Dorkin said.

Rose felt a mixture of shock and relief, but mostly relief — not only that Mullen was not lying dead on the drive, but that the two of them had not done a runner into the sunset.

"Is she alright?"

Dorkin was watching her through narrowed eyes. "Someone drugged her," he said. "Very likely it was your friend Mr Mullen. I was wondering if you knew where he might have gone."

"Why should I know?"

"You're pally with him, aren't you? Maybe he told you. Maybe you're planning on meeting up with him."

"What on earth do you mean? I am a friend. But I don't know where he is. And if, as you seem to be implying, you think I am involved in some criminal activity with him, then why on earth would I have come here when there are police swarming all over the house?" She couldn't help feeling pleased with her own logic. But that didn't stop Dorkin giving her his grade one hard-man stare. She tried to face him down, anger beginning to stir. She hated bullies. Starting with her father, she had always hated bullies.

But Dorkin had not finished. "Let me tell you, lady, that assisting a murderer is a very serious offence."

A murderer? Mullen a murderer? Surely not. She shuddered, but held Dorkin's gaze. "Am I free to go?" she said after a long pause.

Dorkin nodded. "Please do." He was suddenly as polite as pie. "This is potentially a murder scene so we don't want it contaminated. But if you do a runner, make no mistake — we will catch you and we will question you until we get the truth out of you."

Rose turned and walked away, back towards her car. Fear had been replaced by fury. 'Lady!' The word resounded in her head and she felt something not far from hate for Detective Inspector Dorkin.

* * *

Dorkin and Fargo watched Rose Wilby get into her car and drive off down the road in the direction of Wooton.

"So you don't think she's involved?" Fargo said.

"No."

"She likes Mullen."

"She wouldn't have come here if she was complicit with his plans. She's an innocent stooge who's been taken for a ride."

"So where's Mullen?"

"He'll have an escape route. People like him always do. A fake passport. A boat moored in a marina on the south coast under another name."

Fargo looked down at his feet because he couldn't bear to look Dorkin in the eye. It was as if his boss had given up on catching Mullen. Fargo found that deeply disturbing.

"We need to get a marker on his car," Fargo said. "If he's heading for the south, he'll probably have gone down the A34. We'll soon pick it up."

"He's probably changed his car or switched the number plates. He doesn't strike me as being a stupid criminal." Dorkin was up to his thighs in his slough of depression.

Fargo pressed on. "There will be evidence in the house. If he's got a boat, there will be some paperwork somewhere to tell us that."

"You think he's going to leave stuff lying around for us to find?"

"He'll have made a mistake," Fargo said, trying to sound more confident than he felt. Dorkin's gloom was infecting him.

"Fat chance." Dorkin spat into the gravel and pulled a pack of cigarettes out of his jacket pocket. He lit up and sucked in a lungful of smoke before releasing it into the Boars Hill air. He turned towards Fargo. "Well what are you hanging about for then, Sergeant? Get on with it." And he stamped off down the drive.

* * *

Rose Wilby only decided at the last second to pull into the car-park of the Fox pub. It wasn't the call of nature which impelled her to do so, even though she did want to go to the toilet. It was more a case of needing to think and a car-park seemed as good a place as any to do so. She switched off the engine, but made no move to get out of the car. Mullen was a murderer? She couldn't grasp the idea. How could he be? He was too nice. He wasn't the type. Except, of course, she had never as far as she was aware met a murderer, so how on earth could she know that he wasn't the type?

Eventually she got out of the car, walked the length of the parking area and entered the pub. She had been here once before. She went to the ladies, did what she needed to, looked with dismay into the mirror and exited. She stopped in the porch, taking advantage of the shade, and rang Mullen's mobile. It went straight to an answering service. He had turned it off. No surprise there. She was pretty sure that the police could trace you through your mobile nowadays, so it made perfect sense.

What a fool she was to have fallen for a man like Mullen! She began walking slowly down the slight slope of the car-park, reluctant to reach her car because then she would have to get into it and drive back to her flat and then face up to her mother's 'I told you so' and the pity of all the others. Her car was three-quarters of the way down the long row of cars on the right, but when she reached it she continued walking, her pace increasing. Her eyes were fixed on a blue Vauxhall Astra parked at the farthest point on the left, tucked up under the hedge. Most particularly they were focused on a dent on the nearside rear wheel arch. When she reached it she bent down and touched it, reassuring herself that she hadn't imagined it. She straightened up and peered inside. It was neat and tidy as it always was. Her mother often commented on how particular he was. But what on earth was his car doing here? She delved inside her bag, extricated a biro and an old supermarket receipt and scribbled the registration number on the back.

Then she ran back to her car, got in and rang her mother.

"Yes, dear?" It was the tone of voice, patronising and rather bored, that she often used when speaking to her daughter.

"Where's Derek?"

"Derek?"

Rose was breathing heavily. "Yes, Derek. Your lover, Derek." She had never referred to him like that before. Derek was a 'friend.'

"He's gone to the coast. I told you that, didn't I? He's gone sailing for the weekend with some school pal. Archie something."

"Where does Archie live?"

"Well, on the coast of course. He loves his sailing."

"In that case, can you tell me why Derek's car is parked here in Boars Hill at the Fox pub?"

There was a pause. Then a question: "Are you sure it's his, dear? Lots of people have Vauxhalls."

"Of course it's his. I'd recognise the dent on the wheel arch anywhere. I was there when he did it. And besides, I'm sure it's his registration number." She read it out.

Her mother made no reply for several seconds.

"Cat got your tongue?" Rose was aware that she was becoming more unlike herself with every word she uttered, but she had no desire to stop. "Well?"

"There must be a reason. Perhaps he got a lift with someone."

"Ring him and ask him."

"I can't." Her mother, usually so self-assured and bossy, sounded feeble, crushed even.

"Then I will," her daughter continued, undaunted.

"That won't do any good. His phone is turned off."

"What?"

There was the noise of sobbing from the other end of the phone. Rose could barely believe it. Her mother never cried. "He sent a text. He said he had forgotten his charger and his battery was low, so he was going to leave his mobile turned off in case he needed it for an emergency over the weekend."

"Where is he, mother? Why is his car parked here in Boars Hill?"

But the only reply she got was more tears.

* * *

Dorkin was standing by the gateway looking across the fields towards Oxford. The haze had almost cleared and he saw clearly why it was known as the city of dreaming spires. But the view failed to lift his spirits. The fact was that there were few dreams in his line of work — and those he had once entertained lay shattered in his past. He had just finished his third cigarette. He always carried a packet, and often it sat untouched in his pocket for days on end. But when the black dog came barking, it was the only safe solace he could find.

He was about to succumb to a fourth. His fingers were feeling for the filter tip as his eyes continued their hopeless stare across the valley. Then he became aware of a car coming fast from the left, too fast for this stretch of road. He tried to pretend he hadn't noticed. He wasn't a traffic cop for crying out loud! He put the cigarette between his lips and felt in his right-hand jacket pocket for his lighter. There was a squeal of brakes and Dorkin turned his head, alert to the possibility that he might be in danger. A silver Rav 4 rocked to a halt less than a metre away. He recognised it, just as he recognised the woman getting out of the driving seat. He said nothing. She looked as though she would have enough to say for both of them.

"You've got it all wrong!" Rose Wilby had come up so close to him that he edged back half a pace. "Doug Mullen is not a killer."

Dorkin lit his cigarette and took a drag, his eyes taking in every feature of the angry round face in front of him. He exhaled the smoke out of the corner of his mouth. "So you said a little while ago."

"Derek Stanley's car is parked down the road at the Fox."

Dorkin nodded. He deserved this. It served him right for standing out here on the roadside while his colleagues did all the work inside the house.

"You know who Derek Stanley is?" she pressed.

Dorkin nodded. "From your church."

"He's my mother's special friend. That's what she calls him anyway."

Dorkin dropped his cigarette on the ground and crushed it with his left foot. "It's not a criminal offence to park in a pub car-park." He regretted the remark as soon as he had made it. It was hardly going to calm the woman down.

"I've just spoken to my mother. According to her, Derek Stanley has gone to the south coast for the weekend to sail with his friend, Archie. So the question is, what on earth is his car doing parked here in Boars Hill?"

"Are you sure it is his car?"

"Yes."

"There's probably a simple explanation."

It was a bland, patronising statement and it proved to be the last straw. Rose's red face turned deep crimson. "Do I look like a fool, Inspector? Do you think all women are fools? Do you think your rank confers on you a superior intellect above all others?"

Dorkin flinched.

"Derek Stanley has lied to my mother. He has parked his car here in Boars Hill, not more than a mile away from Mullen's house, where a woman has been seriously drugged and from which Mullen has disappeared. Maybe you should consider the possibility that these various facts are interconnected."

Dorkin ran his hand over his thinning hair as he prepared his reply. He knew Rose wouldn't like it. "The most obvious connection is—" But Dorkin never completed his sentence.

"Sir!" A panting Fargo had come jogging down the drive. He was in his white overalls, but his face, like Rose's, was puce. "We've found something."

"What?"

"Two sets of footprints in the garden where the vegetables are. Fresh ones. Almost certainly this morning we reckon." Fargo paused, panting.

"What size?" Dorkin snapped.

"One is size ten and the other size eight."

"Does either match Becca Baines?"

"I've just rung the hospital. She's a six."

"What is Mullen's foot size?" Dorkin demanded of Fargo. The sergeant wiped his forehead with the back of his hand and shrugged. Dorkin turned his gaze to Rose. "Would you happen to know?"

"Ten sounds about right, I'd say. But if you check his bedroom upstairs . . ."

Dorkin swung back to face Fargo, infuriated by the woman's common sense. "Haven't you checked that already, Sergeant? Mullen lives in the house. He must have shoes there unless he has taken them all with him."

Fargo shook his head.

"Then do so."

Dorkin watched Fargo lumber back up the slope towards the house. He could feel Rose Wilby's presence next to him, ready to smile patronisingly and tell him how stupid the police were. If that was what was in her head, he wouldn't blame her. He turned towards her, but there was merely a deep frown that creased her forehead. "My mother bought Derek a pair of shoes for his last birthday. She asked me for my advice." She paused, as if she was making sure of her facts. "I'm almost certain they were size eights."

* * *

Mullen's first conscious thought was that at least he was not dead. His second one, however, was that maybe it wouldn't be long before he was. The fact was he couldn't see a thing. His eyes were open — or at least he thought they were — but everything was black. He listened, searching for clues to where he might be. There was nothing beyond his own breathing.

He tried to remember what had happened. He recalled blundering round the garden, feeling more and more like an elephant on ice. Something had been wrong. He had seen something that was seriously wrong. But then nothing. The word rohypnol floated around his brain. Rohypnol and Chris. Rohypnol and Janice. Rohypnol which knocked you out and expunged your memory. He shut his eyes — or were they already shut? — and drifted back into sleep.

* * *

The depression that had hung over Dorkin like a Thames Valley fog had disappeared, blown gently away by a woman with a round face, dark curly hair and a determination not to go home. He had suggested to Rose that she might like to leave it to them — the 'professionals' was the word he had stupidly used — but her disbelieving look almost made him apologise for the suggestion. He didn't blame her for a moment. He hadn't wanted her to contaminate the scene, so he had taken her away from the Cedars, crossing the main road and entering the grass field opposite. There was a new bench some fifty metres from the gateway and he had led her there. They had sat down and his hand had started feeling in his pocket before he realised that he had no urge to light up another cigarette.

For a minute or even two they sat in silence, looking across towards Oxford, each lost in their own thoughts. And the one thought which kept surfacing at the top of Dorkin's brain was a simple one: I need this woman.

Eventually he broke the silence. "Tell me about Derek Stanley."

"Can you be more precise?"

"What does he do for a living? What does he spend his time doing when he's not working? Where does he live? What I'm trying to work out is where he might be now. He's parked his car at the Fox. He's made his way to the Cedars on foot. Let's suppose that somehow he has drugged both Becca Baines and Doug Mullen. Mullen's car is missing. I am guessing Stanley wants us to assume what we did assume, namely that it was Mullen that drugged Becca — and Chris and Janice too of course — and that now Mullen has done a runner. So what is Stanley going to do next?"

Dorkin paused briefly. It wasn't a proper question, more a case of him thinking out loud, but Rose Wilby answered it anyway. She spoke quietly. "He's going to kill Doug and bury him somewhere he won't be found . . ."

"Or maybe make it look like suicide," Dorkin said. "If he did that, he wouldn't have to worry about disposing of the car. It's harder to make a car disappear without trace than a body."

Rose began to cry. Silent sobs shook her body.

"We can save Mullen if we can find him." Dorkin held out a hope that he didn't feel. "Time is against us, but he's only been missing an hour or two. So I need you to think. The chances are that they are not far away. Stanley will know that if he drives Mullen's car too far, he is at risk of being caught on camera and picked up by us. We will be looking for Mullen's car because we'll be looking for Mullen. Unless Stanley intends to disappear himself, he needs to return for his car so he can drive back home as if nothing had happened. So what I want you to tell me is did Stanley have any favourite places he used to go? A wood maybe. A cottage in the countryside." Dorkin dribbled to a halt. He had run out of suggestions. There was plenty of woodland up here on Boars Hill, he told himself, but there were plenty of big houses too. It was hardly an ideal place for Stanley to hold and kill Mullen. But if they were going to lay on a search, they had to start somewhere — assuming, of course, that he was given the manpower to do so.

Rose Wilby stood up very suddenly and clapped her hands together. "Of course! Savernake Forest. He goes there two or three times a year."

Dorkin looked at her. His first reaction was negative: Savernake Forest was a heck of a long way away if Stanley was intending to make his way back to Boars Hill to collect his own car.

"You remember the Hungerford massacre?" Rose pinioned Dorkin with her intense gaze. "Michael Ryan ran amok in Hungerford. But the first killing took place in Savernake Forest. Stanley's sister was living in Hungerford at the time. She was injured by a shot through her window. Nothing critical, but she was so traumatised that she committed suicide a year later. Anyway Derek goes back there every anniversary of her death. It's like a pilgrimage. He goes other times too. Sometimes he camps out in the woods."

"So he'll know it really well."

"I would have thought so."

Dorkin stood up. "That's where we'll start then. Unless the team have turned up anything else that points towards another direction."

They strode side by side back to the little swing gate, across the road and along the pavement to the Cedars. Not for the first time that day, a red-faced Fargo came hurrying down the drive. This time there was a grin on his face. "Mullen's car, Guv. The guys have got a fix on it. It went down the A34 and then west along the M4. We've got only one sighting on the M4, so they may have exited before they got as far as Swindon."

"Get out of those overalls," Dorkin snapped. "They've gone to Savernake Forest. And we need to organise some back-up."

Fargo stared at him. "Savernake?"

"Don't stand there gawping, Sergeant. We've got a killer to catch."

* * *

Mullen was buried deep underground. He had to be. It was so silent and so dark. He began to feel panic crawling over him, like a giant spider. Oh God! He tried to thrust his head upwards, as far as his bonds would allow, dreading the moment when his head made contact with the lid of the coffin and confirmed his worst fears. Nothing. He tried again, straining even harder to stretch his neck that bit further, but again all he encountered was air. Stale air, but air nevertheless. Air! If he was entombed in a coffin underground, there wouldn't be any air worth speaking of and he would surely have used it all up by now. He would be dead, whereas he most certainly wasn't. He felt an absurd sense of relief, absurd because he knew with certainty that his chances of getting out were virtually nil. He lay back and listened to his own breathing as it returned to normal after his exertions.

He heard another noise. It was a mechanical noise, a scraping sound, a key in a lock he thought. There was another noise, of an unoiled door squeaking open. A light flashed into his face. He shut his eyes and tried to turn away.

"Awake at last."

Mullen said nothing, largely because he couldn't. There was a gag digging into his mouth.

"Thought I had overdone it. Thought I had lost you. The problem was I didn't have a clue how much you'd drink, so I had to put plenty of rohypnol in the bottle."

Stanley giggled. "It was bloody neat the way you both drank it. Couldn't have worked out better! You leave her dosed up on the floor and you disappear. A day or two later a walker finds you here in the woods, hanging from a tree. Your last text message is a single word: 'Sorry.' But it's a word that says it all: sorry for Becca, sorry for Chris, sorry for Janice. As far as the police are concerned, it's case closed."

Stanley moved closer to him and began to loosen the ropes that were holding Mullen captive. "I've got a Taser, so one wrong move and I let you have it in the neck."

Mullen couldn't make any moves, let alone a wrong one. When Stanley told him to get up, his ankles were still hobbled and his hands tied behind his back. He would have to bide his time. There would come a moment when he could make a move. He had to be ready for that split-second opportunity. He had to believe that his chance would come. And yet Stanley's professionalism told him differently. There were no real clues as to where he had been held all this time — nor did Mullen have any idea how long he had been there. All he knew was that he was aching worse than he could ever recall aching before.

Stanley had put a noose round his neck and was leading him by the rope through a door. "If you try anything stupid, I'll burn you alive. Got it? So it's your choice. What sort of death do you want?"

It was dark outside. Not pitch dark, but dark enough. Half-nine or ten Mullen reckoned. So not much chance of running into any dog walkers. He was on his own.

They stopped after Mullen had shuffled maybe a hundred metres. Stanley began to wrap the rope around the branch of a tree. Mullen struggled to understand at first. How could Stanley hang him from there? And then he noticed through the darkness what was on the other side of the tree. Nothing. Empty space. The tree was on the edge of a cliff. Not a Cornish-style coastal cliff, but there was enough of a drop for what Stanley was planning. Perhaps twenty metres. After that there would be only oblivion.

"Do you know why I did it?" Stanley seemed to want an answer. He stood in front of Mullen, keeping his distance, and demanded a response. "Well?"

Mullen thought he knew, but he shook his head. It was a case of anything to delay the end, to gain a bit of time. If Stanley was busy talking, he might let his guard down and make a mistake. If Mullen could get him close enough, maybe he could head-butt him — knock him down and kick him over the edge, though how easy it would be to kick with two feet bound close together and his hands tied behind his back was something Mullen tried not to think about too deeply.

"Chris was a bastard." Stanley spoke clearly and precisely. "He turned up at the church and played us all for fools. A down and out. Fallen on hard times. Disowned by his family. Not that he talked about his family because that would have given the game away. Even so I think Margaret recognised him quite early on. And he knew her all right. That was why he had come to Oxford, to apply a bit of pressure on her. In a word, blackmail. You see, Margaret had had an affair with Chris's father, James, and Rose was the result of that liaison. They kept it secret, but James died six months ago and before he died he told Chris. Perhaps he thought it would be nice if Chris and Rose met up. Or maybe not. Anyway, the fact is that James was a wastrel and by the time his debts had been paid, there wasn't much left over for Chris."

Mullen was watching Stanley closely. He was listening because Stanley wanted him to, but at the same time he was waiting for an opportunity. If only he could induce the man to come really close.

Now that he had started, Stanley was clearly not going to stop until he got to the end. "Chris was a charmer, as his father had been. Everyone in the church was conned, except for Margaret of course. He wanted money, you see. Lots of money. Margaret offered him a little to go away, but a little wasn't enough for him. So he used his charm on Rose. Helping her in church, flirting politely, ever the gentleman fallen on hard times. And Rose, the silly woman, was taken in.

That was when Margaret panicked. The idea of the two of them having sexual relations was just too much. She told me, of course. I was her confidant. She swore me to secrecy and I respected that. But that didn't mean I couldn't do something about it. I didn't tell Margaret. It is better and safer to work on your own. And so I did. After I had killed Chris, Janice got suspicious and started asking questions. That was unfortunate." He paused as he considered what he had said. "Anyway, I had no option but to silence her. And after Janice you came sniffing around." He swallowed. There was a howling noise in the dark and he cocked his head. He smiled. "Just a fox," he said. "It's nothing to worry about."

Mullen lunged forward. It was now or never. Time was running out fast and Stanley had drifted fractionally closer. But Stanley was quick, much quicker than Mullen could be with his limbs tied. The next thing he knew Stanley had tugged at the rope around his neck and he was falling to the ground. His head cracked against something hard and almost immediately he tasted blood.

"Stupid man!" Stanley screamed out the words. "What do you take me for? An idiot?"

Stanley dragged at the rope again. The pain in Mullen's neck was excruciating. "Up, damn you. Say your prayers." Stanley was shouting and Mullen felt saliva spatter across his face. "Your time is up, Doug!"

Stanley yanked on the rope once more. Pain jagged into his neck. Mullen wanted to cry out and say something, but the gag round his mouth was far too tight. Instead he resisted as best he could. Lying on the ground, he began to roll and jerk his body with all his remaining strength. Stanley would have to drag him to the edge. He wasn't going to make it easy for him.

Then out of the darkness came another noise. Not the call of a fox this time, but a sharp crack. It was followed almost immediately by two more cracks as more bullets found their mark. The pressure on Mullen's neck slackened and Derek Stanley slumped to the ground, his body falling like a sack of corn across Mullen's legs.

Epilogue

Mullen was halfway between sleep and wakefulness. He seemed to be sleeping a lot lately. And dreaming. He opened his eyes briefly and shut them again. It was so bright. He didn't mind the darkness. 'To sleep, perchance to dream.' Mullen wasn't exactly the world's most literary person, but the words of Shakespeare floated up from somewhere in his past. His dreams were much nicer than they used to be. No visions of Ben. Not that he could remember his dreams, except as being pleasant, unthreatening. A nurse in a navy blue uniform was the only feature that had stuck in his mind. Or maybe she was real . . .

When he woke next, he opened his eyes and again shut them almost immediately. He had visitors standing at the end of the bed. He didn't feel like visitors. He didn't want to be questioned about what had happened or how he felt. He didn't want to be asked if he wanted anything. Not even when the visitors were Rose Wilby and Becca Baines. If anyone had interrupted his dreams to ask him who he would like to visit him, the two of them would have been top of the list, but definitely not at the same time. The two of them together was far too complicated.

Perhaps they had noticed his change of state for he could sense them moving closer to him along the bed until they stood either side of him. Which one was Becca and which one was Rose he wasn't sure, but he had no intention of opening his eyes to find out. He could smell their different scents. Perhaps he ought to have been able recognise which smell belonged to which of his bedside admirers, but he struggled to be the sort of man who noticed such things.

"He looks cute doesn't he?"

"Like a little boy, all tucked in his bed."

"Bless!"

Mullen wasn't sure he could differentiate the voices, let alone the perfume. Which was pretty ridiculous, he told himself. Maybe this was the consequence of his ordeal — shock or concussion or something.

"Are you sleeping with him?"

"No. Are you?"

Mullen almost opened his eyes at this point. The conversation had taken a distinctly odd and intrusive turn.

"I was briefly tempted," the first one said. "But not for long."

Mullen felt a surge of indignation. "I can hear you," he wanted to say. "It's me you're talking about. Me, lying here on the bed between you, while you gossip about me and tell each other how you've tested me and found me wanting!"

"So you're not interested in him then?"

"I didn't say that. Actually I do find him rather intriguing."

There was a silence. Even Mullen in his dumb state could sense the tension between the two women.

"I really like him," the other one said. That had to be Rose.

"May the best woman win," came the reply.

There was another pause. Then they both burst into laughter.

One of them bent low and kissed him on the forehead. Then the other. After that they retreated out of the room, still giggling together. Mullen opened his eyes and searched for his bell. He rang it. Hopefully the nurse would give him some sympathy. He needed it. He wondered if she would be the navy blue woman of his dreams.

THE END

Thank you for reading this book. If you enjoyed it please leave feedback on Amazon, and if there is anything we missed or you have a question about then please get in touch. The author and publishing team appreciate your feedback and time reading this book.

Our email is jasper@joffebooks.com

www.joffebooks.com

Follow us on facebook www.facebook.com/joffebooks

Please join our mailing list for free kindle crime thriller, detective, mystery, and romance books and new releases. www.joffebooks.com/contact

Find out more about Peter Tickler at www.petertickler.co.uk

14335761R00130

Printed in Great Britain
by Amazon.co.uk, Ltd.,
Marston Gate.